HART'S
Desire

A La Fleur de Love Novella

By

LORI LEGER

LARGE PRINT Edition

ISBN-13: 978-1-940305-43-1

Copyright © 2018 Lori Leger

 CAJUNFLAIR
PUBLISHING

Dedication

To my own hero, my husband, Michael…
Thank you for my happily ever after.
I love you, babe.

Prologue

July 16th, 1975
Dallas, Texas

A single shriek ripped into the silence, echoing through the corridors of the Dallas Texas Home for Girls surgical ward—unofficially known as the Home for Unwed Mothers.

"Make it stop. Please. Make it stop!" Her previous ear piercing screams had long given way to low, exhausted groans.

Seven hours ago, Melinda had decided the word labor was slightly misleading when it came to giving birth. She'd labored in her mother's flower garden, and labored helping her father do yard work. She'd even labored over her homework. None of which came close to this excruciatingly painful experience. Her opinion, vocalized approximately mid-point during the fifteen hour delivery process, had earned a sarcastic comment from one particular stiff backed woman in white assisting the doctor.

"If it were any easier, they'd call it something else."

Melinda had taken time out of her panting to roll her eyes at the self-proclaimed Florence Nightingale of the establishment. She'd also kept her follow-up thought to herself.

You'd think they, whoever the hell they were, could come up with a better description for a day long process of having your insides ripped from you.

"Nobody said it would be a walk in the park, young lady. Remember that, the next time you spread your legs for a b—"

"That's enough!"

The doctor's bark silenced the white clad woman, causing her mouth to pucker as if she'd sucked on a green persimmon. If she could just get to her, Melinda could easily have scratched the old bat's eyes right out of her skull. The urge lasted a full two seconds before another pain lashed out across her abdomen—the worst yet. This one wouldn't turn loose of her.

She panted through it. "Oh God. . . oh Jesus . . . how long is this going to last?"

"Until you give birth," persimmon mouth muttered.

Pain finally got the better of Melinda. "Shut up, you miserable old hag!" She snapped her mouth shut, grunted. No way would she apologize, even though her parents hadn't raised her to be rude. Then again, they hadn't raised her to get knocked up in high school, either. She'd done that all by herself.

Well, not exactly, but he'd been non-existent during all this.

Grant it, her parents had whisked her away in the middle of the night before she could speak to him. God, what a nightmare. She could still see the look on her mother's face once she'd narrowed down her daughter's prognosis. One phone call and two hours later, and the three of them were on their way to Seattle to wait for the next flight to Dallas.

She could understand him being upset that she'd left without a word. She couldn't call—there was one phone in this entire place, and it stayed locked up in an office. But she'd written countless letters to him the past seven months. He'd never bothered to write back, not even one lousy letter. Obviously, he wanted nothing to do with her or their child. But he'd change his mind. As soon as he saw her holding their baby, he'd change his mind. If she could just speak to him, or better yet, somehow get to him.

Another pain caught her mid-thought, this one accompanied by a strong urge. "I feel like I need to push." Her low groan lengthened, turned into a strangled scream.

The doctor's scrub-cap-covered head disappeared under the sheet. After a quick inspection he spoke. "The baby is crowning. When I say to, I want you to push, Melinda." He checked something down there and lifted his head. "Now, push. As hard as you can. Push."

She did. She pushed, and grunted, and screamed through clenched teeth, until finally—finally—something gave way with a warm whoosh, bringing immediate relief.

"Oh God, let me see!"

The doctor and Florence worked on the baby, neither saying a word. She heard a strangled mewling sound, started to panic.

"What's wrong? Is my baby all right?"

"Just have to clear the mucus . . .she'll be fine."

Melinda caught the raised eyebrow, a silent message from nurse to the doctor.

She had a baby girl? She heard the sound of suctioning, then a tiny cry of protest. Then another, this time louder.

"Let me see. I want to see her."

Still they huddled around the child.

"What's wrong?"

The woman sent her a glare. "He's clamping and cutting the umbilical cord. It's procedure."

She allowed herself to relax a little. That lasted until Flo turned away from her, clutching the child. Panic filled Melinda suddenly as the woman blocked her baby from view.

"Bring her to me."

Only silence greeted her as the doctor turned back to work under the sheet. She barely noticed him. Her eyes were glued to the too white crisply starched back of the nurse's dress.

"Give me my baby!" The ear piercing shriek bounced off the sterile, white tiles of the tiny delivery room.

Florence spoke in the stern, heartless voice so many girls at the home abhorred. "We can't do that, Miss Dawson." Her voice sounded muffled through the mask covering her face. "It's against regulations."

"Whose regulations?" Melinda demanded, trying to sound stronger than the grueling experience had left her. "That's my child." Desperation filled her seventeen year old mind as quickly as water in the hull of a leaking boat. "I want to see my baby. Now." The nurse continued to ignore her as she swaddled the child Melinda had just forced out of her exhausted body.

When the woman pivoted toward the door with her baby, Melinda let loose with belligerent screaming that caused everyone in the room to freeze in place.

"For crying out loud," the doctor yelled as soon as she stopped to take a breath. "Let her see the baby so I can work on her in peace before she hemorrhages to death."

"She's not supposed to. Her parents insisted it be given up as soon as—"

"I heard him say I had a girl. My daughter is not an it, and I want to see her now!"

The young mother held her breath until the nurse turned reluctantly toward her. She pulled off her mask and carried the tiny bundle wrapped in yellow to her. Yellow. It was the only color in the too-white room, from her perspective of flat-on-back-feet-in-stirrups, anyway. The look of sour disdain on nurse Flo's face had Melinda wishing the old witch had kept her mask on a little longer.

She stretched her arms to their limit as the nurse hesitated just beyond her reach. "Give," she demanded, determined she'd have this woman fired as soon as she could get out of here with her baby girl. Florence Handley had been a miserable pain in her butt since the day of Melinda's arrival at the home.

Melinda took the bundle carefully and settled it on her belly. She pulled the blanket aside and gasped as she peered down at her daughter.

"Hello baby girl," she breathed, reaching up to pass a finger along downy soft skin of the infant's cheeks. "You have my hair." She stared at a head full of damp, dark locks that would surely curl as she grew. "You have my nose and mouth, too." She moved her forefinger to the tiniest cleft below her daughter's bottom lip. "But you have your father's chin," she whispered, smiling through her gathering tears. "Our daughter has your chin," she croaked hoarsely to the one person missing from the scene, wishing she could speak to him for one minute. The instant she squeezed her tear-filled eyes shut, Flo seized upon the opportunity and ripped the infant from her arms.

"That's enough. You should never have seen the child in the first place."

"Nooo! Give her to me. I want her," she pleaded. The door shut, blocking out the view of the woman as well as her child. Horrific screams filled the air. Hysterical and physically weakened, it shocked

Melinda when she realized it came from her. She fought to get up, suspecting that if she didn't get to her daughter tonight, she'd lose her forever.

The doctor cursed, raised one hand flashing a glove covered in crimson. Even as the blackness closed in on her, Melinda took note of the bright red blood standing out in stark contrast against the sea of white.

Blood on his hands.

"Oh God, she's hemorrhaging. We're going to lose her if we don't stop this!"

The doctor's voice sounded far away, muted, barely penetrating through her consciousness.

Her last thought ... she'd be glad to die.

No baby.

Nobody to love.

No reason to live.

Chapter 1

June 4th, 2005

Gregory Hart cringed at the too damned cheerful jingle of his electronic shop's front door. The last thing he wanted to deal with right now was another customer. It was Friday afternoon before a much needed weekend, and all he wanted to do was to go home and pop a top on an icy longneck. He clamped his jaw tightly at the sound of feminine footsteps approaching but didn't look up from the spreadsheet on his computer screen.

Days like this . . . hell, weeks like this made him want to pack up and sell the place. Just take off and drive somewhere, anywhere else in the world. Anywhere but here, where every direction he turned, something or someone reminded him of the wife he'd lost to cancer a year ago.

A woman spoke from the end of the aisle to his left. "Excuse me, where do you keep the batteries?"

"Do you know the size you need?"

"They're for a television remote control. Uh, triple-A, I think."

Keeping his eyes on his spreadsheet, he reached up to the counter display on his right and pulled a pack. "Will these do?" He slid the pack to the end of the check-out counter.

"That's just what I needed. What do I owe you?"

That voice. Something about the woman's voice sounded disturbingly familiar—tweaked something locked up in his memory banks far longer than he wanted to admit. He looked up, and his gaze landed on a pretty lady with curly reddish brown hair. She perused the pack of batteries and nodded. Her sparkling green eyes met his gaze briefly before she started digging for something in her purse.

His breath left him in a rush the moment recognition dawned. He stood speechless, staring at the woman who'd left town as a young girl of seventeen, taking his heart with her. Thirty years had changed her, of course, but not enough to keep him from knowing the first woman he'd ever loved.

"How much do I owe you?" she repeated, sounding breathless and rushed for time. He'd heard a rumor once that she'd been in Texas all these years . . . Houston area. Judging by the prominent accent, more fact than rumor.

"I'd say you owe me about two bucks—and one broken heart. Not sure I can put a price tag on that, though." She froze, standing there with her hand shoved deep inside her purse. "You're looking good these days, Melin."

Her head pivoted slowly, her wide-eyed gaze locked onto his, shock keeping her speechless. Her pupils dilated seconds before her cheeks flushed a becoming shade of pink he'd seen many times before.

Some things never changed.

"Gregory?"

He lifted one brow and nodded. "That's right. What brings you back to this part of the world?"

"My-my mom passed."

"I'd heard. I was out of town when it happened. I'm sorry for your loss."

She stammered, sounding a little flustered. "D-da-dad needs me here to take care of him."

"So, what you're saying is, this isn't a visit, but a relocation?"

"For the time being, anyway. How long have you been back in McCray? Last I heard you'd joined the Marines."

"I retired with twenty-five and came back in 2000. I figured I'd given the U.S. military enough of myself, and it was time to live my own life. I married a year later."

"You hadn't married before then?"

She seemed surprised. At what? The fact that he hadn't waited for her?

"Nope. I kept waiting to hear you'd come back to town . . .but you never did." He pointed one finger at her. "You're the reason I made a career of the Marines." Her face paled, and just for a millisecond, he thought he should feel guilty for making the comment. Her reply made him swallow the apology he'd considered.

"I guess that makes us even, then. You're the reason I never came back." Her words were the ultimate insult. An icy proclamation of bitterness and anger.

Before he could reply, she'd spun on her heels and walked out, leaving the batteries there on the counter. The only sign she'd even been there was the echoing jingle of the door's bell and the lingering fragrance of Chanel No. 5.

Some things definitely never changed.

Melinda Dawson slammed her car door, blocking out the sound of everything but the hammering of her heartbeat. Greg Hart—the man who'd left town without leaving any kind of message for her. Who'd never written her back the entire time she was at the home. Never sent a letter to either her, or her parents' home to let anyone know how to contact him. Nothing. And he had the nerve to accuse her of breaking his heart?

"Well, ain't that a kick in the teeth?" she murmured. It took several tries to get her shaking hands to slide the key into her car's ignition.

Her peripheral vision caught his tall form standing in the doorway, watching her peel out and away from the curb in front of his shop.

How the hell had she managed to end up in the one shop, with the one person in town she didn't want to see?

Dad.

"I need batteries for my remote, Mel," she mimicked, repeating her dad's complaint first thing this morning. "They're special batteries I only get from McCray Electronics. Could you go pick some up for me?" Melinda snorted in disgust as she pulled into her dad's drive three blocks away.

She stalked inside her childhood home, closing the door firmly behind her and throwing her keys in the bowl on the snack bar. The sight of her dad relaxing in his recliner flared-up her anger all over again. "You know, you could have warned me, Dad."

"About what?" Lawrence Dawson asked his daughter, looking innocently unaware that he'd set her up.

"That Greg Hart works in the electronic shop."

"He doesn't work in it, he owns it. Adele Hayes works in it."

She narrowed her eyes suspiciously at the man who'd grown frail during the thirty years she'd spent in Texas. She could count her visits home on one hand in all those years. The number of times Greg's name had been mentioned during those infrequent visits had been zero.

"Well, he was sure as hell there this morning." She crossed her arms tightly, still feeling the sting of Greg's totally un-called for comment.

"Really? Hmmm, hope Adele's not sick or something. Since your mom's gone I don't get to hear the scuttlebutt around town. Don't know who's sick or on vacation or what. So, where are my batteries?"

Melinda dropped her head and cursed.

"Nice language for a lady. If your mother were here—"

"She's not, Dad. And you're lecturing me on language? Really?" She fished her car keys out of the bowl and headed back outside.

"Dammit!" She slammed her car door again and threw her purse on the seat. Her car's engine roared to life, punctuating a single thought. She'd drive across the state for batteries before she'd voluntarily face that man again.

She pulled into the parking lot of the only anything-but-super super market in her tiny home town. By the time she'd thrown her keys in her purse and gripped the door handle, a large hand landed with a slap on her closed window.

"What the hell?" She pushed her door open, staring in annoyance at the damp hand print on her previously spotless driver's side window. She swung the door wide an instant before a pair of laced boots and jean-clad legs blocked her from stepping out of her car. Two seconds later he was squatting before her—eye to eye. She sat there staring, for the second time that morning, into the face of Greg Hart.

Thirty years had changed the boy into a man, put lines around his eyes that weren't there before, and peppered his hair with streaks of silver. Damn if it didn't make him look better than he had at nineteen years old. She thought of the box of Nice and Easy she'd bought last week to touch up her roots. Pictured it, sitting in the bathroom cabinet at her dad's house, and grew irritated all over again. Some days it just sucked so bad being a woman in a man's world.

She lowered her chin and glared at him over the top of her twenty dollar sunglasses. "Are you stalking me?"

"I'm a retired Marine, Melin. If I wanted to stalk you, there isn't a damn thing you could do to stop me. But no, I'm not stalking you."

"Move out of my way."

He didn't.

"Are you trying to push me into calling the cops?"

He shrugged. "Go ahead. I'll get out of it." He held up two fingers and grinned. "The mayor and I are this close. Besides, I just came to bring you these. I figured you were picking them up for your dad." He threw them on the seat and stood.

"We may not be the big metropolis of Houston, Texas, Ms. Dawson, but we still do things like that for each other around here." He spun on his heel and headed away from her.

She didn't catch her breath until he was several feet away from her. "Hey!" she called out. "Since you're flaunting knowing the mayor in my face, who is this lowlife you're so tight with? You know, just so I'll know to vote for the other candidate come election day."

He stopped and turned slowly to face her, wearing the most irritatingly sexy grin she'd seen on a man in a long, long time. He slapped his chest twice with both hands then extended his arms. "You're looking at him." He bowed at the waist.

The mild expletive exploded from Melinda's mouth before she could stop herself. She frowned as she heard the deep rumble of a chuckle coming from the smug man she would have died for so many years ago. Refusing to let him get the best of her, she stared up at him. "Wait, I still owe you money for the batteries."

He took one step back, then another, still facing her. "You owe me for a lot of things, Melin. Maybe we could take it out in trade one of these days."

The sexist comment had her seething inside, wanting to slap that smug grin right off of his face.

Instead, Melinda kept her cool. She picked up the four-pack of batteries and stood, facing him. She flung it at him in a precise arc that landed at his feet.

"Keep it, Mr. Hart. I'll buy some while I'm here."

"But you're going to pay twice as much as I'd charge you," he called after her.

She turned, throwing a comment over her shoulder. "And it'll be worth every last cent."

She walked in the house and tossed the bag of batteries to her dad, still seated in his recliner. "Here's your damn batteries, Pop. I practically had to mortgage the car to do it but it's done. Jeeze, the super-market here is expensive."

"Well, why the hell didn't you buy them from the electronics store like I told you? As far as I can tell, everything the man sells is reasonable."

She stopped and faced him, hands on hips and still fuming over Greg Hart's nerve. "I'm not interested in a damn thing that man is selling, thank you very much."

Her dad shrugged off her comment, didn't even bother firing back a "suit yourself" or "whatever floats your boat".

Melinda decided not to feed the beast any further and opened the side by side's freezer section to study its contents. "What do you want for supper, Dad?"

"I don't know, honey. I'm not all that hungry lately. All this medicine I'm on—makes every damn thing taste the same."

She lifted her head to study him. Her dad had always stood taller than his five foot nine inches, straight backed and solidly built, slightly on the stocky side and full of energy. The man seated in the chair had lost a considerable amount of mass the last several years. She'd grown accustomed to those gradual changes with every brief visit over the years. This recent loss of spark in his eyes unsettled her even more—a clear sign of the pain he felt over having to bury his wife.

Determined to bring him a little enjoyment by way his palate, she grabbed a pack of ground sirloin from the freezer. "How about I make up a batch of my special lasagna. You loved it the last time I baked it for you."

Her father harrumphed. "The last time you made it I could probably still taste. These days I can't distinguish the difference between marinara sauce and applesauce." He shook his head. "I've got a mind to quit taking all these damn meds. Just die at home in peace, enjoying my food the way God intended me to."

She approached his recliner and gave him a one-armed hug from behind. "No, you won't. You've still got some living left to do. I'm here to help you out."

He lifted one hand to pat her arm gently. "I appreciate you being here, honey—I truly do. But there's a difference between living and existing."

Melinda gave her dad's neck one last squeeze before straightening. She approached her parents' cast iron sink with the package of meat. The stark contrast of red on white jolted painful memories long pushed aside—bright red splotches of blood against the sterile white surface of a surgical ward. She released a long sigh, as always, revisiting the wave of helplessness she'd felt then and many times since.

This moment proved no different from any other, with her thoughts lingering on a single tiny bundle of yellow. Many times she'd set out to find her baby girl, only to face insurmountable road blocks of one kind or another. She'd never put the loss behind her, rather had learned to live with the situation, accepting it as God's will. Wherever her daughter had ended up, God had intended her to be there for a reason—to meet her perfect match, have her own children, and start her own family. She imagined that somewhere out there, she had a daughter, a son-in-law, and maybe a grandchild or two. And maybe one day, God would see fit to reunite her with them.

Melinda clung to that image, gleaming a small measure of comfort from the scenario. She had no choice, really.

The alternative would be too impossible to bear.

Chapter 2

"**M**elin! It's so good to see you. Get in here, girl."

Melinda hugged the woman she'd been buddies with since first grade. Even a few brief visits during their two thousand mile separation hadn't put a stop to their friendship. She stepped inside. "This place is gorgeous, Cyn. Look at that classic detailing." She ran her hand along the carved wood trim of the door frame and wainscoting. "Is this original to the house or due to a remodel?"

"Oh, please. You know I don't have a creative bone in my body. That's your thing, not mine. We bought it just the way it is, but we've worked hard at giving this place that 'lived-in' look."

Melinda laughed at the tiny blonde with big blue eyes. "God you look good, girl. I bet you haven't gained an ounce since high school. How do you stay looking so young?"

"I run."

"Really? Like marathons and events like that?"

Cynthia shook her head. "I run my daughter to dance line practice, to softball practice, and gymnastics. I run my son to track and swim meets. I run back and forth for Matt's dry cleaning, I run to the store, I run to pay bills and keep food in the fridge. Those kids eat me out of house and home. And when they bring their friends over, it's even worse. I swear I'll have to take out a loan just to keep them fed soon."

"Yeah, right—Mrs. 'I married one of the most successful orthopedic surgeons in Washington State'."

Cynthia put her head back and laughed. "Honey, those kids can cut through a paycheck like a hot knife through a batch of summer honey. If you had kids, you'd kno...Oh...I mean." She sucked in her breath, obviously embarrassed at her remark. "Melin, I'm so sorry."

Melinda smiled sadly and placed a comforting hand on her friend's arm. "It's okay. Don't worry about it."

"I don't think sometimes," Cyn said, as she slapped at her own head. "I just talk and talk without thinking a thing through, sometimes. Abigail calls it diarrhea of the mouth."

"I said not to worry about it. Now show me the latest shots of your gorgeous kids. How old are they now?"

"Abigail is seventeen and just finishing up her junior year. This time next year we'll be gearing up to send her off to college. Jacob is fifteen and he'll be a sophomore next year."

Melinda followed Cyn to the latest school shots of both teenagers and gasped. "Oh, my gosh. They're both so grown up. How did that happen so quickly? It seems like a couple of years ago they were still toddlers."

Cyn pulled a bottle of wine from the cooler and set two glasses beside it. "I know, right? They were babies when those two you were taking care of both left for college." She put a finger to her temple. "Tiffany and . . ."

"Drake," Melinda finished for her. "Doctor Tiffany LeBlanc is a surgeon at a hospital in Lake Coburn, Louisiana. And Mr. Drake LeBlanc, Attorney at Law, is practicing law in his father's firm right there in Houston." She smiled at the thought of the two children she'd raised and loved since they were both infants. "I probably should have moved out of that big old house the day Drake left for college, but Daniel begged me to stay on to tend to things when he's gone. And he's gone . . . a lot."

"And Daniel is..."

Melinda sipped at her wine. "Daniel LeBlanc, my employer, is Tiffany and Drake's father. He's a fine man, even though he's got his priorities a little screwed up when it comes to his kids. But he's a lot better than their mother, the Wicked Witch of West Houston."

Cynthia, who'd uncorked the wine, poured them each a portion and carried the glasses to one overstuffed couch as Melinda followed. "Now, you'd been a live-in nanny to those kids since their birth, is that right?"

Melinda made herself comfortable, then grabbed the glass and nodded as Cyn sat beside her. "Tiffany was under two months old when Daniel's mother hired me. Now she was a nice lady. She taught me everything she knew about children, and believe me, she knew a lot."

"So, you and this Daniel..." Cyn's brow crinkled in curiosity. "You two...never...you know." She wiggled her eye brows suggestively.

"Of course not! That was the best job in the world. No way was I going to ruin it by doing something that stupid. Besides, those two are still married even if they can't stand the sight of each other. They're both members of the ultra-rich and snooty Houston society crowd. He's ultra-rich and she's ultra-snooty. Neither one of them had time to pay any attention to those poor kids." She shook her head. "Trust me, Cyn. Living with those people taught me how not to treat children."

"You really were like their mother, weren't you?"

Melinda placed a hand over her heart. "I love those kids like they're my own. I'm so proud of the adults they've become, and I know I've helped them get there. There isn't a mean bone in either of my two babies." She wiped a tear from the corner of one eye and took a deep breath.

"Do you still see them?"

"I did, and often, up until two weeks ago. Drake made it a point to come by a few times a week if I cooked his favorite meals for him. Tiffany, not so often, but at least one weekend a month." She ached for them, as much as any mother separated from her children by several states.

"Things have been moving so quickly lately, I haven't had a chance to let you know what's been going on." She took a deep breath to speak the words it had been so difficult to follow through on. "I'm home, Cyn. Or at least until dad . . ." She paused, despite the lack of closeness between she and her dad, not wanting to utter those awful words. "Until I'm not needed anymore. After—after that happens— well, I'll have to figure that out when the time comes, I suppose." She met Cyn's sympathetic gaze. "Dad's not well."

Her friend's face fell. "It's his heart, right?"

Melinda nodded. "There's not much they can do at this point. And truth be told, I don't think he wants to do anything to prolong his life since mom's gone."

Cyn's brow wrinkled in confusion. "What about for his daughter—for you?" It seems like he'd at least want to stick around for you. To strengthen that father-daughter bond while he still has the time, at least a little."

Melinda gave her friend a sad smile. "I guess we haven't been that close—not for thirty years anyway."

"But, you two should be working on making those ties stronger now, before it's too late."

Melinda stared at the friend who'd had the constant love and affection from both her parents. Parents who hadn't robbed her of her of the only chance she'd ever had to have a child of her own. "Trust me, Cyn, there's too much water under that particular bridge."

Cynthia reached over, placed a hand on Melinda's, forcing her into some serious eye contact. "I'm right here. Talk to me."

Melinda's eyes clouded immediately. "It hurts too much to talk about it."

Cyn gave Melinda's wrist a light shake. "Maybe it hurts so much because you've kept it pent up inside all these years. Maybe if you do, you'll feel better."

Melinda shook her head slowly, staring into her friend's blue eyes. "It won't do anybody any good by talking about it. Not right now, anyway."

Her friend released an exasperated sigh but sat back against the arm of the couch, as though resigned to go for now. "Well, I still say there's hope. And I don't care what brought it about, but I'm thrilled to have you back in this corner of the country."

"Oh, I'm back, all right. Dad needs me here, so..." she put her hands out. "Here I am; forty-seven years old and living back at home with my father."

"Are you looking for a job? Because City Hall is looking for a clerk and I could talk to the mayor for you," Cynthia gushed. "You know who the mayor is, don't you?"

Melinda stiffened at the mention of the town's political leader. "Um . . .yes, as a matter of fact. I ran across him at the electronic shop yesterday afternoon." She ducked her head and fiddled with the ring Tiffany and Drake had given her before she moved away for good. It bore three different colored diamonds—a different stone for each of them and one for her.

"Greg owns the shop, and he's mayor of McCray too. Isn't that something? Who'd have thought when you left here your senior year he'd join the Marines then come back later to become mayor?"

"Who'd have thought?" Melin repeated quietly, still fiddling with the ring.

Cyn sat up suddenly. "Wait! Weren't you and Greg . . . that's right, I'd forgotten that you and Greg dated for a whole year. I'm sure he'd approve it if you applied, as close as you two were . . ."

Melinda watched her friend falter as the puzzle pieces came together slowly. She took a deep breath before giving Cyn a reluctant smile. "That was a long, long time ago. And besides, I'm not looking for a job. I'm here to take care of Dad, and that's a full time position."

Cynthia chewed at her bottom lip. "I seem to keep putting my foot in my mouth. Talking about things that make you uncomfortable."

Melinda waved off her apology. "Ancient history, girlfriend, so don't let it bother you." She tried to carry off a nonchalance that became increasingly difficult under Cyn's scrutinizing gaze.

"You know, he didn't join the military until you'd been gone for six whole months. He hoped you'd come back after graduation. I remember attending his going away party the weekend before I left for college."

Melin kept quiet, hoping Cyn would keep talking. As much as she hated to admit it, she was curious about the good looking boy who'd grown into such a drool-worthy man. Had two decades in the Marines changed him for the better or made him even worse of a person than he was before? No way could she admit, even to her oldest, dearest friend, how attractive she found him. Truth be told, he still turned her insides to butter.

"He came back here twenty-five years later, all buff, bronzed, and brawny when every other guy his age was going bald and sporting a gut," Cyn continued. "Put these locals to shame, I tell you," she admitted, with a chuckle and a shake of her head. "My brother in law owned the local gym then, and he said his memberships quadrupled after Greg came back and signed up. The men wanting to compete against him, and women wanting to compete for him. He married K'Lynn Roberts a year later. You remember K'Lynn, don't you? She graduated five years after us, a truly sweet girl."

"I'm glad for him. Sounds like he's happily married." Speaking the words didn't stop her from feeling just a little sick to her stomach.

"Oh, but, she died a year ago. As a matter of fact it was a year yesterday because her sister placed a memorial in the weekly newspaper."

Melinda whipped her head up to stare at her friend. "I had no idea. What happened?"

"Ovarian cancer. They'd been trying to get pregnant and by the time they went in to see what the problem was, it was already at stage four. They'd only been married two years when they discovered it. One year later she was gone."

"Oh, how horrible, Cyn. He didn't mention it yesterday. But then, he wouldn't, would he?"

"I guess not. It's more the kind of thing he'd want to forget, rather than remember, isn't it?"

"So, he doesn't have kids from any previous relationships?"

"Not as far as I know. After being married to the Corps for twenty-five years the guy comes back, finally finds somebody and WHAM! Lousy luck, huh?"

Melin couldn't keep the bitterness from her thoughts. Was it luck? Or was it karma, stepping in to kick his ass after a twenty-five year free ride? She'd place her bet on Karma.

Even so, it disturbed her to think his wife had lost her life to pay for his mistakes.

Mom's Fruit Tarts

Dough Recipe (Can be used with any fruit filling and easiest to work with if made a day ahead and chilled):

2 cups sugar
4 cups flour
1/2 tsp. nutmeg

1/2 tsp. cinnamon

1 tsp. baking powder

2 sticks butter, softened (not melted)

2 eggs

½ cup milk

2 tsps. Vanilla extract

Mix dry ingredients first. In separate bowl, cream sugar and butter, then add eggs and vanilla and beat well. Add the dry ingredients a little at a time until it's all added and dough is right for rolling. If dough is too stiff, add another egg. Chill the dough in the refrigerator. Break off small pieces of chilled dough (about the size of an egg) and flatten into a circle. Add filling, fold over and crimp edges. Bake at 350 degrees on greased pan until light golden brown...about 20 minutes or so. (It's not rocket science, Melinda and all ovens do not bake the same way!)

Melinda stared down at the hand written recipe card. The once bright purple ink fading fast against a formerly white card, now yellowed with age. Her mother's neat penmanship written in an old fashioned fountain pen she'd given her mom as a gift one year. The plastic pen casing had been sky blue with bright yellow daisies and had come with matching stationary paper and envelopes. She'd thrown in extra purple ink refills as part of the gift. Melinda remembered well, the look on her mom's face as she opened the Mother's Day gift from her only child. Brenda Dawson had made a big deal out of the fact that the pen wrote in purple ink, her favorite color.

That had been her junior year of high school, and it had been the last Mother's Day they ever spent together. The thought of returning to celebrate that occasion had seemed so fundamentally wrong once her own child had been taken away from her. As any dutiful daughter, she'd always sent a card and promised to visit soon.

Her first visit home hadn't occurred until well after her child's fourth birthday had come and gone…wherever she was.

It had been three year old Tiffany, the little girl she tended to, who'd made her decide to take the trip home. She and Tiffany had been trying their hand at making homemade tarts in the kitchen, and had failed miserably. Covered with flour and bubbling with laughter, she'd been overwhelmed by fond memories of doing the same with her own mother.

She'd called her parents that night, as she had a handful of times over the past four plus years, but this time, she'd discussed a trip home. Her parents had met her at the airport where Melinda returned their eager hugs with stiff ones of her own. They drove her to the family home to begin the grueling task of putting the past behind them.

The first two days of her visit had been uneventful. She and her parents had been reserved with each other, though not cold; their mannerisms slightly strained, without quite reaching the point of being painful when in each other's presence.

No one spoke of her time at 'the home', not a single reference—ever—lest someone discover the dark shroud of secrecy her parents had carefully constructed for their family. As long as it was their secret, her parents could pretend it never happened. Likewise, if they never spoke of it with her, they could pretend she'd been the perfect daughter.

By the third day of her week-long stay, Melinda began looking for the tart recipe. Determined not to ask her mom for help, she'd been searching for hours before Brenda Dawson finally asked what she was

looking for. Her admission had brought a bright smile
to her mom's face…the first genuine smile of the
trip.

"Oh I don't use a recipe," her mom had admitted,
before giving her a hopeful look and continuing.
"But, I bet if we whip up a batch right now, I could
come up with one for you to bring back to Texas."

They had done just that. Her mother had pulled
out her 'special pen' she'd kept in a kitchen drawer
and a pack of blank recipe cards. The result had been
the start of a healing process that had come close, but
sadly, never quite been completed. She'd gone back
to Houston, made the tarts, and had even sent
snapshots of Tiffany and her during the process, as
well as eating them afterwards.

Melinda glanced up at the photo collage her
mother had framed and hung on her kitchen wall.
Beside it was a plaque that read,

*"Good recipes and love…they both last forever if
shared with others…"*

An airline may have brought Melinda's physical
presence back to McCray, but it was a mutual love
for baking that acted as a stent in the clogged arterial
path back to her mother. Somewhat improved, but
never what it was in the past, it was all it could be

considering the history between them. Unfortunately, she'd had no such connection with her father.

His anxious call from the living room jolted her out of her reverie.

"Melinda! Somebody's at the door!"

"I hear, Dad. Can you get it? I'm kind of busy," she called back, her hands and apron full of flour and pastry dough.

"Melin! Someone's at the door!"

She rolled her eyes as she grabbed the dish towel from the table and headed for the door, trying to wipe some of the flour from her hands. She glared at her dad, stretched out on his recliner like a king. She fairly growled as she reached for the door knob. "Don't get up, dad. I can see how busy you are," she said, pulling the door open and staring at their 'visitor'.

Greg stood there, looking ever so much more Marine than small town Mayor, even considering his khakis, royal blue polo shirt, and a Town of McCray baseball cap. The smirk on his face did nothing but irritate the hell out of her.

"Oh, Christ on a cracker. What the hell do you want?"

Greg sucked in his breath, somewhat startled by the sight of Melinda in full Betty Crocker mode. Who the hell knew he'd find a woman wearing a red apron such a turn on? The thing looped around her neck, crisscrossing behind her to tie in the front and cinch the apron around her trim waist.

Obviously startled by his appearance, she swiped at her cheek with the back of her hand. He curled his fingers into a tight fist, his effort to keep from reaching up to wipe away the smudge of white powder her actions had left behind.

Damn, she looked good—despite the scowl she turned on her father, who sat in his recliner a few feet away.

"Dad, what did you do?" she demanded.

Mr. Lawrence turned toward the door, wearing an innocent expression that didn't fool anyone.

"Come on over here, boy. I'm having television trouble. And hurry up 'cause I can't miss my Price is Right, dammit to hell."

Greg turned his smug expression on Melinda and tipped his cap. "Excuse me. I've got business to tend to." He turned his back on her and strode toward the man and his television set.

"What's going on here, Mr. D?"

"This darn old set is getting too old, boy. It's hard as hell to change the channels and sometimes the picture won't come in at all. I thought if I changed the batteries in this remote it would fix the problem, but it didn't."

Greg examined the remote and cast a glance Melin's direction. "Maybe it's just crappy batteries."

Melinda's eyes narrowed with irritation. "Oh, whatever."

He pulled the batteries from the remote. "Can't trust 'em if they weren't bought in my place." She turned to leave the room, snapping her dishtowel loudly and leaving a dusting of flour where she stood.

"Let's see what we got here," Greg murmured, as Melin disappeared into the kitchen. He turned back toward the problem remote, while inhaling the delicious aromas of something along the lines of fresh baked cookies or pies. "There's some pretty friggin' good smells coming out of that kitchen, Mr. D."

"Yep, she's baking again. She says it calms her."

"Oh yeah?" Greg looked toward the kitchen and the sound of slamming cabinet doors. "Why does she need calming?"

"Beats me. She was fine when she got here. But the last three days she's been antsy as hell. Maybe she's going through the change."

Greg chuckled and shook his head. "I wouldn't let her hear you say that if I were you." He switched out the batteries in the remote, but still couldn't get it to work. After a good twenty minutes of checking out the remote and the television, Greg had the problem piece narrowed down.

Melin's dad walked over to meet him carrying a plateful of baked goods. "How's old faithful coming along?"

"Well, it can be fixed, but I'll have to order some parts. This set's over twenty years old." He watched as the older man seated himself carefully in the recliner, mindful of his plate and glass of milk. "I sure hope you planned on sharing some of that."

The old man chuckled. "Here, try this, boy. You've never tasted anything so good. It's her specialty."

"Mr. Dawson, you think you could call me something other than 'boy'?" He reached out for some kind of fruit-filled tart.

"Well hell, boy, what d'ya want me to call you? Shithead or Jarhead?"

"My name's Greg." He bit into delicate strawberry-filled pastry and rolled his eyes in bliss. "Oh man, this is so good."

"I know. I told her she should go into business selling this stuff. One thing she learned how to do in the lone star state was cook. Nobody beats those southerners when it comes to cooking."

Greg couldn't argue with that. He'd spent lots of time vacationing in the south during his stint in the Marines. He'd had the best damn Tex-Mex and melt in your mouth steaks in south Texas, savory seafood dishes in Louisiana Cajun country, some of the best biscuits and gravy he'd ever eaten in Alabama, and everything in between. "I've gotta agree with you. The south does it right when it comes to cooking." The old man nodded and seemed to choose his words carefully before speaking again.

"It's been a long time since you've been here, hasn't it, Hart?"

Greg furrowed his brow at the man's usage of his last name. He shrugged, deciding it was better than the alternative. "Yes sir, it's been awhile." He munched slowly on the tart, watching Lawrence Dawson's eyes mist over as he spoke.

"You know, for while I'd forgotten. Melinda going over there and seeing you at the shop brought it all back to me. She was some kind of upset with me for sending her there. I couldn't remember why, until you got here. Yes sir, it brought it all back, and not in a good way."

Greg swallowed his bite and frowned, wondering what had upset the old guy to such an extent. "What do you mean, sir?"

"Sometimes adults can do some pretty stupid things. Even though they think they're doing them for the right reason, it still doesn't make it right."

Greg cocked his head a little to the side, still as confused as a two-partied politician. "You lost me, sir. I must have missed something along the way."

Lawrence nodded his head slowly. "I know you did, Hart. I know you did."

"Whatever those were, they were damn good."

Melinda stopped crimping tart crusts long enough to spare a glance at Greg leaning against the doorjamb holding her dad's plate and glass. He walked casually into her kitchen like he owned it and placed the dishes inside the dishwasher. When he straightened and looked back at her she returned her attention to her pies.

"Where'd you learn to bake like that, Melin? Were you a professional chef?"

She tightened her lips, determined to ignore him and hoping he'd go away. His presence set her on edge like nothing else. Him hanging around here like he was king of the kitchen made her want to scream. "My mother. Did you fix his remote?"

He stood at her elbow, near enough so the scent of his cologne reached her, totally masculine and clean smelling. She had to concentrate hard to cut out another set of circles from the pie dough and fill one side of each circle with fruit. With a skill born from years of practice, she folded and crimped the tarts and spaced them evenly on her perfectly seasoned baking stone. By the time she grabbed the stone and turned, Greg had opened the oven door for her. She placed the stone in the oven and straightened, somehow having the presence of mind to set the timer. Unfortunately, it took her three tries to get it right, before pushing out an impatient sigh through clenched teeth.

"No," he said.

"No? No what?" she asked, confused at his comment.

"No, I didn't fix the remote. The problem isn't the remote; it's the twenty year old set. I'll order the parts but I left him a loaner until then."

She frowned at the prospect of him paying them yet another visit. "I think I'll just buy him another one. Who keeps the same television set for twenty years?"

He snorted. "You looking for a way to piss off your old man, you go right ahead and do that."

She lifted her chin. "It's none of your concern what I do. Are you finished here, or what?"

He jutted his chin toward the platters of tarts. "Your dad wants a couple of those in a plastic bag."

"Why?"

He lifted one shoulder in a carefree shrug. "I'm just doing what I'm told."

Melinda placed three tarts, one of each kind in the bag. Before she could seal it, Greg cleared his throat.

"I think he said he wanted two of the strawberry ones."

She added another strawberry to the bag and handed it to him before following him to the living room.

Greg made his way to the front door, raising the storage bag in one hand and saluting her dad with the other.

"Thanks a lot, Mr. D. I appreciate it."

"Anytime, Hart."

Melinda sputtered in protest as Greg turned and gave her a wink before walking out and closing the door behind him.

She turned on her father. "Anytime?"

Her dad looked up from the 16" television set Greg had left with him. "Somebody's gotta help us eat all those pies. You're baking enough in there to feed an entire battalion of men."

She crossed her arms and leaned one hip against the twenty year old couch. "I told you, baking calms me."

"You ever thought there might be another treatment for what's ailing ya?"

"Ailing me?" she asked, wrinkling her nose. "Come on, Pop. What's it been since you moved here from Alabama? Fifty-five years?"

Her dad nodded and gave her one of his 'take it or leave it' faces. "Yeah, well, I was watching Dr. Phil the other day, and he said that one of the symptoms of growing older is that you often revert to the way you were in your younger days. Just be glad I'm not suckin' on a bottle and crappin' my pants." He chuckled at the face she made. "I'm sure that'll come soon enough," he said, shaking his head. "Poor you."

Melinda dropped her hands to the side and turned back toward the kitchen. "Yeah, poor me."

She entered the kitchen and sat with the stack of recipe cards. The image of Gregory munching down on her strawberry tarts created a sudden aversion to baking them. She couldn't not bake. She was too unsettled. So it was on to something else. She flipped through the cards, scanning each of the well-worn, time tested recipes, and finally settled on one.

Apple Cinnamon Muffins

1 1/2 cups flour
3/4 cup sugar
1 1/2 tsp. baking powder
1 T. cinnamon
1/3 cup milk
1/3 cup butter, melted
1 egg, slightly beaten
1 cup finely chopped apples
Mixture of brown sugar and cinnamon (1tsp. cinnamon to 1 cup of brown sugar)

Heat oven to 375 degrees
Combine flour, sugar, baking powder and cinnamon in medium bowl. Add all remaining ingredients and stir just until flour is moistened. Spoon batter into muffin liners and top with sprinkling of brown sugar and cinnamon mixture. Bake about 20 minutes.

Chapter 3

Melinda waved at Cyn through the plate glass window of the café before pushing through the door. After giving her friend a quick hug, she settled in the chair across from her.

"These are for you." She pushed a plastic container across the table to her friend.

Cyn lifted one corner of the container and peeked inside. Her eyes drifted shut as she breathed in the delectable aromas escaping from the container. "Are these your mom's tarts? Oh my gosh. I loved the strawberry ones. Please tell me they're not strawberry, or I won't be able to resist!"

Melinda sucked in and made a face. "I could, but I'd have to lie."

"Oh damn!" She reached inside the container and broke off a corner of one tart, popped it inside her mouth. Her eyes rolled in pleasure. "You make them just like your mom did, Melin. I always ordered a couple of dozen of these from her around Christmas, you know. My husband hides them from me and the kids because they're his favorite."

Melinda laughed. "Poor Blake. Make sure he gets a few of those, will you?"

"I'll do that. He'll be thrilled—it's not even Christmas. You'll spoil him. So, how's your dad?"

"The same. Plans his entire day by his TV schedule. Talk shows, game shows, nature programs, war documentaries, evening news, and more nature programs or war documentaries." She checked off her fingers, one by one. "I don't dare sit with him or make a suggestion. So I bake."

Cyn sealed the container and pushed it to the opposite side of the table surface. "Well, we seriously need to find you another past time or Blake and I will both be big as a house. You can join spin class or Zumba with me."

Melinda grimaced. "Ack . . . no, thanks. Classes bore me, and so do gyms. I like my evening walks to keep in shape. I just haven't started them up again since I've been back." She left out the reason she hadn't was to avoid running in to Greg again. It seemed that everywhere she turned lately, he was there.

"Hello ladies. How's it going today?"

She cringed at the voice, knowing without looking up that he'd managed to find her, yet again. Had the man slipped some kind of tracking device into her pocket or her purse without her knowledge?

She looked up reluctantly and met his amused gaze. His comment was accompanied by a smug grin.

"Really, Greg?"

"It's a small town, Melin, and this place has the best lunches around. I swear I'm not stalking you."

She kept her silence, her only other reaction being a slight lift of a single eyebrow.

"I'm here almost every week day. If you're trying to avoid me, this won't work. I'm just saying." He turned to her lunch mate. "Tell Blake the game is on for Saturday, Cyn. Have a good lunch, ladies."

Melinda lowered her gaze to the table top, her jaw clenched with the effort it took not to watch him leave their table. In the end, she failed—looked up to stare at his broad shoulders and long waist, tapering down to lean hips and firm backside. Cyn's voice cut through her thoughts.

"What the hell was that?"

She jumped at her friend's comment, took a deep breath and picked up a menu. "I'm not sure I know what you're talking about."

"Melin . . ."

"What?"

"You two—the sparks—the animal attraction—whatever the hell you want to call it—it's still there."

"It's called history, Cyn. One that won't be repeated, I can promise you that."

"But, you're both single, as well as available—and obviously still attracted to each other."

She grabbed her purse, aggravated that she couldn't argue that point with her friend. But she didn't have to stay here, while he gloated over upsetting her. She stood, looped her strap over one shoulder and left the café as gracefully as she could.

Cynthia caught up with her on the sidewalk. "Melin, wait! What the hell is going on between the two of you?"

"Nothing's going on, Cyn. I'm not young and stupid anymore, that's all. Gregory Hart failed as my Prince Charming thirty years ago. I'll be damned if I'm going to give him a snowball's chance in hell of disappointing me again."

"I don't understand."

"That's right. You don't. I had no way of knowing he'd be there for lunch, but you knew." She pointed at the plate glass window but kept her eyes on her friend. "If that was a set-up, I'd sure as hell appreciate you never doing that again."

"Set up? Jeeze Louise—It's like he said, it's a small town. We have one café that happens to have fabulous luncheon specials."

Waves of guilt washed over her at the sound of hurt in her old friend's voice. Even worse, she looked up at the window and found Greg Hart sitting at the counter—watching their exchange. Even more infuriating was the shit-eating grin spread across the man's face.

Too upset with herself for accusing Cyn, but still too pissed with Greg to resume their lunch plans, she mumbled a quick apology and turned away. She threw back a quick promise to reschedule before climbing back into her car.

She didn't have the pleasure of seeing Greg for another week. Due to eavesdropping on a phone conversation between her dad and his new best friend, Melinda had been able to miss him the day he repaired the old set.

Considering the microscopic size of McCray, she wasn't all that surprised when her luck at avoiding him ran out again.

The front of her grocery buggy had barely cleared the end of the aisle before the screech of metal meeting metal ended in a minor crash of carts.

"Whoops! Excuse me," the deep male voice drawled.

She peeked around the corner to see Greg standing there wearing a sheepish grin. "I should have known."

He shrugged. "It was an accident, and I apologized."

She jerked on her cart to dislodge it from his and turned away without a word.

"Hey, Melin, is there a reason you're so damn rude to me, or are you just a naturally bitchy person?"

Melinda halted mid-stride and pivoted. "Most people think I'm pleasant to be around. It must be you that brings out the worst in me." Before he could reply, she headed for the check out.

It wasn't until she'd unloaded her groceries that she realized she'd left without purchasing flour, her main purpose for the shopping trip.

"Dammit!"

"What's wrong now?"

She turned to face her father. "I forgot the flour."

"You want me to go back?"

"No."

"I can go for you, I don't mind."

"You can't drive."

"Says who?"

She sighed. "Let me rephrase. You shouldn't drive."

"Again. Says who?"

"Says your doctor."

"She didn't tell me that."

She leaned back against the counter, crossed her arms as she met her father's gaze. "Your cardiologist hinted that your dizzy spells could affect your reflexes, and hinder your judgment when it comes to driving skills. She suggested that I do the driving from now on."

"Hinted, could, suggested—none of that sounds cut in stone to me."

She reached over to open the desk drawer and pulled out a stack of traffic citations. "I'm pretty sure the McCray Police Department is in agreement. You've got quite an impressive collection of tickets here, dad." She began to read them off, like a bucket list of things not to do.

"Failure to yield, failure to maintain control, running a red light, side swiping a patrol vehicle . . ." She lifted the stack. "Shall I go on?"

He waved her off. "Ah, what the hell do they know? Petty crap, every bit of it."

Petty? Pulling the side mirror from a police cruiser? Her gaze darted from the oven to her collection of recipe cards, then back to the oven. She needed to create something, anything . . . if she couldn't bake, she'd lose her mind. Melinda pushed off from the counter and grabbed her purse.

"Where you going?"

"To get flour. I'll be right back."

Within five minutes of entering the store, she'd checked out. She walked to her car, toting her reusable shopping bags containing ten pounds of flour. She threw the bags in the backseat of her car and shut the door. She turned, came face to face with Greg."

"Dammit!" She stepped back, her hand placed over her heart. "What is it with you?"

"Why is it that I bring out the worst in you, Melin?"

"What?"

He stepped forward. "I'm curious about what you said in there earlier. I'd like you to answer my question. Why do you hate me?"

"I don't hate you." He took a step back. Seemed to be the slightest bit relieved at her answer.

"So answer my question, then. Why do I seem to be the only person who brings out the worst in you?"

"Leave me alone, Gregory." She tried to turn away. Wanted nothing more than to retreat into the safety of her car. Go to her mom's kitchen and bake until old heartaches took a back seat to the comforting homemade aromas she created. He placed his hand on her shoulder and turned her to face him.

"So, why is it, Melin?"

"I don't know." She brushed his hand off. "Maybe it's because when I needed you most you ran off—"

"I needed you too—"

"You ran off to go play G.I. Joe!"

Greg's jaw tightened, and for a moment she thought he'd walk away without a word.

"Play?" he asked quietly. "You and I must have huge differences of opinion when it comes to games. I lost a hell of a lot of good buddies during my twenty-five year 'play-date'."

"I just meant tha—"

"But thanks for your support, Melin," he said, cutting her off sharply. "It was always nice knowing we had people like you in our corner. I'm sure that attitude of yours would be a big comfort to families of all those dead Marines." He turned on his heel, taking his full shopping cart with him.

She watched his straight-backed, stiff-necked retreat to the opposite end of the store and wondered if she could feel any smaller than she did at this moment.

Strawberry Muffins

2 1/4 cup sifted all-purpose flour
1/3 cup granulated sugar
1/4 cup brown sugar
3 tsp. baking powder
1/2 tsp. salt
2 eggs
1/2 cup oil
1/2 cup milk
1 tsp. vanilla
1 cup sliced strawberries

Stir together flour, sugar, baking powder and salt. Beat eggs and blend in oil, vanilla, and milk. Add liquid to dry ingredients, stirring just until blended. Fold in strawberries. Spoon mixture into paper lined muffin tins. Top with 1 tsp. of strawberry preserves (OR any fruit preserves of your choice) and bake at preheated 375 degree oven for 25 minutes.

July 16th

Melinda pulled down the last jar of her mother's strawberry preserves from the pantry and studied it closely. Barb Dawson's prize-winning preserves, containing some secret ingredient that she claimed made hers stand out from the rest. She held the jar lovingly to her chest. "What was it, Mom?" she whispered, wishing just for once, her mother had bothered to write down this particular recipe. "It would mean so much to me if I could make it just like yours." She examined the jar, willing it to reveal its secrets to her before placing it back on the shelf. She couldn't bear not to have at least one jar of the preserves left to treasure.

Backing out of the pantry, she pulled several jars of store bought preserves from her reusable grocery bag. Granted, they weren't as good as her mom's but they'd make some pretty tasty muffins, and she needed to bake. Her father's comment came back to her as clearly as a high priced sound system.

You ever thought there might be another treatment for what's ailing ya?

She rubbed her forehead with the back of her hand. "The cure would be to find my baby girl, Pop," she whispered. But the chances of that happening were slim to none. God, if she had a quarter for every night she'd cried herself to sleep thinking about her, feeling the weight of her newborn child in her arms, even though they were empty. She'd never forget the sight of her. Her hair, her nose, the tiny little mouth, and his chin.

She'd looked. God had she looked for her child. On her eighteenth birthday she'd gone to the orphanage, the one the grapevine of rumors said they brought the babies to. The woman behind the imposing desk told her she couldn't do a thing without a lawyer. From that day on, she saved her tips from waitressing but even at the end of six months it wasn't enough for a retainer.

Shortly after that, she got the position with the LeBlanc's, with a significant salary increase. She easily saved what she needed as a retainer fee for an attorney. For the first time, she had hope. Daniel LeBlanc had even given her the name of a good lawyer. She'd never forget the day he'd told her about the orphanage being destroyed by a fire. It had started in the very section of the building they kept the records. Nothing had survived. Her one consolation at the time had been that no child had been hurt in the fire. But since then, every trip to an orphanage, adoption agency, or any other state agency had ended with her walking away empty handed.

Her daughter, thirty-one years old today, was most likely alive somewhere, but Melinda wasn't any closer to finding her than she was the day she was born.

Melinda stepped inside the pantry, and shut the door. There, hidden and alone, she sobbed—reliving the heartache and pain of losing the only child she would or could ever have. The emptiness within her always seemed more pronounced this one day of the year—on her daughter's birthday. It seemed especially sharp this year, maybe because Greg was so near, a constant reminder of his abandonment.

Every time she saw the man he'd grown into, she felt torn. She'd loved the boy once, but he'd betrayed her, without so much as a phone call or a letter. Each sight of him was like a fresh slap in the face. He'd chosen freedom over her, and for that, she could never forgive him.

If only she had someone to talk to about this. Nobody, other than her parents, knew she'd given birth, not even her closest friend.

Years later, she'd admitted to Cyn that she'd gotten pregnant and her parents had shipped her off to the home. But somehow, speaking to anyone other than Greg about the baby's birth felt wrong. Instead, she told Cyn that she'd miscarried, and due to complications, she couldn't have any more children. The last part was true, unfortunately.

She ached inside, wondering about the only child she would ever give birth to. Where was she, how was she, was she married, or had she made her a grandmother yet? Had she been happy with her adoptive parents?

She couldn't bear to watch the horror stories about orphans and foster children who'd slipped through the cracks of the system to be abused, or worse, by adults they should have been able to trust.

Every day she'd prayed her child wasn't among them.

Melinda took a deep, restorative breath, and stepped out of the pantry. She'd barely had time to wipe her eyes and blow her nose when her father called from the living room.

"Melinda! There's someone at the door!"

She bent low over her reflection in the mirror-like chrome surface of the toaster, and groaned. "For once, could you get it?"

"Nope, got my hands full."

She pushed through the kitchen's squeaky old swinging door and froze in her tracks. Her father truly did have his hands full, this time, with a twenty year old television set that had to weigh fifty pounds if it was an ounce.

"Dad! Are you trying to throw out your back? Or worse?" She rushed to help him. Together, they lugged the heavy set to the kitchen table from the rickety stand that had supported it for two decades.

The old man waved off her concern. "I could have handled it by myself. I'm not a damn invalid, you know."

"If you hurt your back and can't get to the bathroom, your journey from adulthood back to infancy may be quicker than you think. Adult diapers are not out of the question."

"All you gotta do is take me out to the back yard and hose me down."

Melinda cringed. "God, that's an image I don't want burned into the old memory bank."

"That's what I used to do to you if you'd crap your pants when your mother left me to watch you for a while. You loved it!"

She backed her way to the door, pointing at him. "Adult diapers, Dad. I'm just sayin'!"

She pulled open the door to reveal Greg standing there, looking particularly well dressed for an 'appliance business' house call. He gazed down at her wearing that crooked grin of his—the kind most guys try to perfect in their teens while standing in front of a mirror. Melinda knew Greg's came naturally. She'd admired it since her first day of kindergarten when, as a much more mature second grader, he'd helped pick up the spilled contents of her book sack.

Her heart had carved out a special niche for him that day, and it had remained there—until a mother's heartbreak had taken its place.

"Who needs diapers?" Greg asked, his voice filled with amusement.

"Nobody yet, damn it all!" Lawrence Dawson shouted. "But I will be soon if she keeps treating me like a baby. When I was young I could have carried two of those sons a bitches. One in each arm," he bragged, pointing to the old set sitting on the table.

"You didn't haul that there by yourself, did you, Mr. D.?" Greg intercepted a look from Melinda that gave him his answer. "I told you I'd move it and haul it off for you once I set up the new one."

"What's going on here?" Melinda asked. "I thought you'd fixed it already. Do you have to bring it in to work on it?"

Greg shook his head. "What I did before was a temporary fix, but when I checked out the parts online, I realized it would cost nearly as much to fix the thing as it would to by a new one." He pointed at a box leaning on the side of the porch rail. "I've brought a nice, new flat screen for him to try out. If he likes it, I'll give it to him at my cost."

Melinda frowned. "I'll pay the retail price for it. My days of needing any help from you are long gone."

Her father turned and pointed a finger at her. "Hold on a minute, missy. You're not paying for this, I am, and if that boy wants to do me a favor I'll say 'thank you' and take it."

Tight lipped, she pivoted and rushed back into the kitchen. Normally, she left the doorstop under the kitchen door to keep it open. Under these circumstances, she kicked out the stop and let it swing closed behind her. "Pralines." She grabbed her stack of recipes, muttering under her breath. "As soon as those muffins are in the oven, I could make pralines. And fudge. Yes . . . definitely fudge."

Lawrence shook this head at the door swinging back and forth after his daughter's disappearance. "She's going through the change, I tell ya. Her mother, rest her soul, gave me an ass-chewing every day for two years before she settled into it."

Greg emitted a low whistle. "I think it's just me she hates, and one of these days I'm gonna find out why. She's the one that broke it off when we were kids. Hell, she up and moved to California with no explanation except that she couldn't tell me to my face she didn't give a rat's ass about me."

He turned and froze when he saw the look on the older man's face. "You okay Mr. D.? Damn, you didn't hurt yourself carrying that old set, did you?" Lawrence blinked several times before meeting his gaze.

"No, I didn't hurt myself, but you and I need to talk about a serious matter, Hart. Too much time has gone by as it is."

Greg glanced at his watch. "Nothing would make me happier if it'll shed some light on the situation, but I sure as hell don't have time for it today. As soon as I set this up, I have some mayor business, a ribbon cutting ceremony at the newest hair salon in town."

"Hmmm boy. Sounds like a wild afternoon."

Greg lifted the box containing the new set with one hand. "It's not all bad. I get free eats," he said, patting his belly with the other.

"What the hell's in there?"

"This is your new 36 inch flat panel LCD screen television set."

"You're shittin' me, right?"

Greg chuckled. "No, sir, I'm not. Everything you need is in this box—built in HD digital tuner and everything." He watched the man stare from the box to the dinosaur on the table and busted out with a hearty laugh. "Welcome to the world of modern technology, Mr. D."

Pecan Pralines

(Drake's favorite…especially for dropped catch, game-losing days!)

4 cups sugar (1/2 white, 1/2 brown sugar)
1/2 stick butter
1 lg. can evaporated milk
1 tsp. vanilla
2 or 3 cups pan roasted pecans

Cook all ingredients except nuts until it reaches softball stage. Add pecans, beat, and drop by spoonsful onto parchment paper.

Note to self: Drake likes them without pecans, Tiffany prefers hers with walnuts.

Old Fashioned Chocolate Fudge

(Broken Heart Fixing/Stress-Reducing Chocolate Therapy for Tiffany)

2 cups sugar
2/3 cup milk
1/2 cup cocoa
1/8 tsp. salt
2 T butter
1 tsp. vanilla
2 T light corn syrup

Put sugar, milk, chocolate, salt and syrup in heavy pan and stir over low heat until dissolved. Increase heat and boil steadily until it reaches softball stage. Remove from heat and add butter and vanilla. Beat until creamy and pour into buttered pan. Let cool and cut.

Note to self: Tiffany prefers hers either plain or with walnuts. Drake prefers his with pecans.

Chapter 4

Lawrence Dawson did a slow shuffle from his second nightly trip to the bathroom on his way to the kitchen. He couldn't remember the last time he'd slept through the night without having to get up to drain the old lizard. Damn prostate. Good for nothing but making an old man feel even older. Figured as long as he was up he'd steal one of those muffins.

He stopped in front of the swinging kitchen door, the one his wife had insisted on him installing when they bought the house in 1960. He pushed gently letting it swing to and fro. He stood there for a while, letting the memories flood his mind. He stared at the door, painted a soft yellow, and tried to remember the last time it had been closed. Once the cancer had started sapping his wife of strength, he'd kept it propped open. It was easier to get the wheel chair in and out without banging up her knees. After she passed, he'd seen no reason to remove the door stop. Once he got sick, he'd seen even less reason.

But today, for some reason, Melinda had seen fit to let the damn thing swing loose, closing herself inside the kitchen for hours. Something had set her off. Or someone—Greg Hart, no doubt. Bad business, that.

He cleared his throat, pushed open the door and stepped inside the kitchen. He pivoted in a circle and released a long, slow breath. Every surface area in the kitchen was covered with baked goods and confections of some kind. Tarts, muffins, cookies, and her recent additions—and even more disturbing—pralines and fudge.

"Holy shit, are we in for it now."

For as long as he'd known his wife, when she'd been feeling down, her drug of choice had been sugar. If combined with chocolate, an even more effective combination.

Clearly, Melinda had inherited her mother's little idiosyncrasy.

But what had happened to send her into the sugar tailspin? Surely it wasn't just Greg's appearance today? Shaking his head, he opened the cabinet door to grab a glass for some water. The calendar hung just inside the door on a tiny nail, exactly where Brenda had always kept it. He looked closer, squinting at something written in the square. He flipped on the light over the sink to get a better look at it. Someone, Melinda he presumed, had drawn a pink heart to encompass the square of yesterday's date. Inside she'd printed a neat #31.

He did the math, immediately realizing what had thrown his daughter for a loop. Not only was it her daughter's birthday, but its father had shown up on their doorstep as a reminder. The man she believed hadn't cared enough about her and the child she carried for eight and a half months.

Only he knew better. He, and three other people, all gone now.

The four of them had made serious errors in judgment that had haunted all of them since. Here it was, three decades later, and he was the only person alive who could set things right. The plot had involved two sets of parents, all working together, determined to keep their children's reputations from being tarnished, their futures bright—open to possibilities of college and careers.

He shook his head, wiped at the tears in his eyes. Instead, they'd all lost. He and Brenda, their only daughter to a life in Texas. The Harts had lost their son to the Marines. They'd all lost a grandchild. As it turned out, the only one either couple would have.

Was that God's punishment for lying to their children all these years? The price they had to pay for their choices? His parish priest said God didn't punish that way, but Lawrence wasn't so sure. As a matter of fact, if he was a betting man, he'd say that's exactly what happened. Looking back on it, he knew they got exactly what they deserved. That, and more.

But Melinda and Gregory had lost more than any of them. They'd lost not only the chance to love and know their baby girl, but they'd also lost each other in the bargain.

He pulled the calendar from the nail and sat heavily at kitchen table. The table where he and his wife had shared too many meals alone, without their daughter—their baby girl. He dropped his head in his hands, forcing himself to revisit every painful detail of that awful day, as well as the months that followed.

Poor Melinda had suffered through the worst possible experience she could have gone through. And she'd suffered through it without either of her parents around.

They'd planned to be with her for the birth, had planned to make the drive to Dallas a week before the due date. Instead, Melinda had gone into labor two weeks early. They'd left immediately, drove non-stop other than bathroom breaks and the occasional meal. By the time they arrived, some thirty-five hours later, Melinda's baby had already been born and taken away from the home. That's when they discovered there had been complications—severe enough that their daughter had come out of the surgery unable to have children.

They'd stayed by her side for two days straight as she slipped in and out of consciousness. The first words out of her mouth had been for her daughter. She'd wanted to hold her. Begged them to bring the baby to her.

In light of everything that happened, he and his wife had discussed the possibility of reclaiming the child. But how could they do that? How would they explain arriving back at McCray with their daughter and a new baby? How would they explain that they'd kept her hidden away for seven months? How would they explain away the lies, the cover story they'd already told their friends, and everyone in their town?

No, they had to see it through—for the sake of their daughter. Especially since Gregory Hart had up and joined the Marines to get over his own heartbreak.

Knowing she wouldn't be recovered enough to travel for two more weeks, he'd purchased his daughter's airline ticket and left it with her. Four days later, they'd started their long drive home, expecting to have Melinda use the ticket to fly home a week and a half later.

He'd never forget that morning she was supposed to board the plane to Seattle. Brenda had gone to Sunday morning mass when the phone rang. He'd accepted the collect call from Dallas, suspecting her flight had been delayed. The conversation was burned into his memory.

"Dad?"

"Melinda. Did your flight get delayed?"

"Something like that."

"What do you mean?"

"I'm not flying home. I cashed in my ticket."

"Wh-what do you mean?"

"I bought a bus ticket instead."

"The bus? Are you sure you're well enough to ride a bus all the way home? It could take days."

He'd never forget the pause she'd taken before sending their world into turmoil. Her answer had been like the proverbial kick in the gut.

"I'm not going home."

"Melinda, what are you saying?"

"I can't go home without my baby." She paused again, seemed to think better of it. "I won't go home without my baby."

"You listen here, young lady—"

Her tone was hard, determined. "No. No, I'm not listening to anyone else anymore. Thanks to you and mom, my baby girl is gone. You did nothing to stop it, even after you discovered this was my last chance to have a child of my own. I can never forgive you for that."

"We did it for you, for your future."

"You did it to avoid the embarrassment of having a daughter who got knocked up, a grandchild born out of wedlock."

"Your reputation would have been ruin—"

"This wasn't about my reputation. It was always about yours and mom's. God forbid the Catholic Daughters and Knights of Columbus find out you don't have a perfect daughter."

"Melinda, that's not fair."

"You want me to be fair? After you let those people take my child away from me? And all because the two of you were afraid of a little gossip." She laughed then. "It's ironic how you both have always said you wanted grandchildren. And because of your unwillingness to be seen as anything other than perfect, you've lost the only grandchild you'll ever have. I hope you're happy, because now you've lost your daughter too."

"Melin—"

"I only called to tell you I'm not going home. I've got a bus to catch."

With a single click of the phone, she'd disappeared.

Fools. The four of them had been such fools, thinking something like that could ever work out. How could they have not seen the disaster waiting for them? How could they have believed their daughter would ever find a way to forgive them?

They didn't hear from her again for another six months. Even then it was only to tell them she was working in a café, and still didn't have her daughter. She was quick to add a bitter "Thanks to you two," before slamming the phone down in the middle of their explanations. He'd never forget the look on his wife's face, standing there with the kitchen phone extension in her hands, staring blankly at him. He'd hung up the living room extension and rose from his chair to meet her. Before he got to his wife, she'd turned from him, ran to lock herself away in their room for the rest of the afternoon.

As bad as that call had been, it was nothing compared to the heartbroken bout of tears and accusations the third phone call had produced. She'd been working for the LeBlanc's for six months and had her own attorney. The one thing she knew was that her child had already been adopted. But the orphanage had burned down, along with any and all records of the children who'd been there.

"Why didn't you get her back, dad? Once you and mom knew . . .why didn't you go to the orphanage and get your only grandchild back? I'll never understand it." She'd stammered broken sentences through her heartbroken sobs. "I know Greg doesn't care, but I never expected my own parents not to care. I thought at least her grandparents would find it in their hearts to love her."

"Oh Melinda, we do love her, and we love you. We only want the best for both of you."

"I'll never understand your kind of love," she'd sobbed.

Brenda had grabbed the phone from his hands, uttered a desperate plea to their daughter. "Come home, baby. Please, come home to us so we can work through this. Take some time off, think about which college you want to att—"

He'd already rushed to the second extension by then. He got to hear Melinda laugh, cutting off his wife's comment, as well as her reply to that suggestion.

"Home? You think I'd feel at 'home' over there with the two people who've betrayed me the way you have?"

"Melin—"

"No mom! This is how it has to be. I'm not going home to you and dad. I'm not sure I ever can. There's a baby girl right here who needs me. Tiffany LeBlanc is not my own flesh and blood, but her mother is a cold-hearted bitch and I'm going to do whatever I can to make sure she grows up feeling loved."

He'd spoken from the extension. "Your mother only meant—"

"I don't want to hear it, dad. Be thankful that I have enough fond memories of my own childhood, that I felt loved enough to give baby Tiffany that same experience. I know I'm thankful for that." She paused briefly before twisting the knife. "I'm just sorry you couldn't find that same love in your hearts for my child."

Brenda's gaze had locked onto his through the two doorways separating them. She'd covered her mouth with one hand—stood there, silent, and wearing an absolute look of horror. She had to have been feeling the same kind of soul-crushing heaviness as he did at that moment.

"Maybe—maybe I won't always feel this way, but right now, I do. I've got to go now. Tiffany needs to be fed and put down for her nap." She'd ended the call then. Neither of them realized it at the time, but it would take another year for Melinda's pain to dull enough to call them back.

It had nearly destroyed his wife—nearly destroyed their marriage. But through couple's counseling with their parish priest, they'd survived it, finding a way to channel their guilt into helping other needy children. They worked with existing charities, established new ones to help raise money for the orphanage in Seattle, for various homes for children across the state.

It was their therapy. Just as raising another couple's children, first tiny little Tiffany LeBlanc, and later, her brother, Drake, had been Melinda's therapy.

Lawrence stared at the calendar, rubbed his thumb over the pink heart. He pulled a handkerchief from his pocket and wiped his eyes. "Poor Melin. No wonder you locked yourself in here all afternoon."

He stood slowly, feeling his seventy-eight years as he'd never felt them before. Hanging the calendar where he'd found it, he left the kitchen, heavy hearted, but more determined than ever to find a way to make it up to his daughter.

Even if it was the last thing he did on this earth.

Greg knocked again, louder this time. The door swung open, revealing a rumpled looking Lawrence Dawson. "Hey, I just wanted to swing by and see how you're liking that new flat screen."

"You're kidding, right? What's not to like? Picture's twice the size of what I had before, the color's fantastic, and it hardly takes up any space."

Greg beamed at him. "Just what I like to hear— another satisfied customer." He lifted a box. "I also brought the wall mount kit I told you about. I've got time to hang it for you today, if you'd like."

The old man cocked his head to the side before throwing the door open. "Sure, you can. I still can't believe they make such a thing. If someone had told me fifty years ago I'd be watching a skinny television set that was hanging on my wall I'd have said they'd cracked their noggin."

"Technology can be a beautiful thing, Mr. D." He walked over to the set with the box. "You want it on this wall?"

"Yup."

"Greg opened the box and removed the metal brackets. He glanced toward the closed kitchen door. "Is Melin in there baking again?"

"No. She took off about an hour ago. Said she had some errands to run and wanted to go to the library to do a little research on one of their computers."

"You mean she doesn't have her own? Hell, I couldn't function without a computer at work. Tell her she needs to get herself a nice little tablet style computer, or at least a laptop. It's probably all she needs."

Mr. Lawrence gave him an incredulous look. "So she can stay even more cooped up than she already does? Hell no. She needs to get out and see some people."

"I see your point, Mr. D."

The old man stood. "You want something to eat, Hart? I'm getting myself a little something while she's not here to fuss at me."

"She got any of those strawberry tart things left? If so, I won't turn one of those down. I worked through lunch."

"Coming right up."

Greg had the bracket attached to the wall already by the time Mr. D returned, carrying a plastic container under one arm and two glasses of milk.

"Here you go, Hart. I fixed this up for you to take with you. She's adding candy to her collection."

Greg tightened the last screw onto the bracket on the back of the flat screen. "Her collection?" He lifted the set and attached it to the wall bracket before turning back to him. "What do you mean?"

Mr. D. lifted the lid on the container and pushed it toward him.

Greg examined the contents with a low whistle. "I see what you mean. She must need some hellacious calming down. Either that, or she's going into business for herself." He bit off a bit of a praline and rolled his eyes. "Oh man. She could too, with all this stuff. There isn't a thing in here I wouldn't be willing to pay for. The bakery building is still empty. You ought to talk to her about re-opening the place. I know it's up to the new building codes."

The old man nodded. "I hadn't thought of that, Hart. I'll do that. Or you could tell her yourself—If you happen to run into her at the library when you leave here."

Greg nodded slowly at Mr. D., wondering what the old fart was up to. "I guess I could, at that. Although I don't know why I'd want to subject myself to the tongue lashing she always seems to have waiting, especially for me."

The serious look Mr. D. sent him had Greg wondering about the cause of it.

"Oh, I've learned over the years that some things are worth subjecting yourself to a little discomfort. Take it from me, Hart. You don't want to waste too many years before you figure that out for yourself."

Greg rounded the last corner of the DIY section of the library and saw her seated before one of several computers set up for the patrons to use. He stood right in front of the monitor and still she remained focused on whatever she saw on the screen.

"What's got you so interested you don't even see me, Melinda?"

With two clicks of the mouse, she shut down the site she'd been on and closed the notepad in front of her. "Why are you here?"

"You know, I offer a couple of laptops and pads you might be interested in. What are you researching?"

"I-I was looking up some recipes."

"Seems like you'd have plenty of those already."

She stood, slipped the notepad in the side pocket of her purse before looping it over her shoulder. "Not that it's any of your business, but I was looking for heart healthy recipes for dad."

"Good luck getting him to stick to a healthy diet."

"He'll stick to it if it's all I cook for us. Anything more complicated than peanut butter and jelly sandwiches, or toast is above his kitchen abilities."

"You might have to cut back on your baking. He sneaks it every chance he gets, you know." Her face didn't reveal a thing. "And speaking of your baking, I was just telling your dad that the only bakery in town shut down a few months back and it's still empty. I know for a fact the building's up to code. Have you thought about turning those skills of yours into a business?"

She stopped, as though weighing the situation, then shook her head. "I can't think about that right now. Not with dad."

He stepped around the desk to meet her. "Well, it's something to think about, anyway. Maybe in your future?" He looked around, making sure they didn't have an audience. "Would you like to go to dinner with me sometime? Or even a cup of coffee maybe?" He reached out to brush a lock of hair from her forehead, frowned when she flinched and pulled away from him. "What, Melinda?" He shook his head. "What the hell did I ever do to make you hate me?"

Her gaze narrowed on him just before she gave a hysterical snort. "You're joking, right?"

"No. I'm not. Ever since you came back to town you've had a pissy attitude towards me, and for the life of me, I can't figure out why."

Her eyes glazed over for a moment before she lifted her chin. "I'm actually a little sad for you, Greg. But not enough to make the same mistake twice. No. I will not go to lunch, or dinner, or even coffee with you." She turned, walked out of the library without a backward glance.

He stared after her, basking in the lingering scent of her perfume. He started to walk away, then stopped, turned back toward the computer. Maybe there was a chance. "Let's see what had you so damn captivated, Ms. Dawson."

The Marines had taught him lots of skills, some not so useful in civilian life, but the computer skills he'd accumulated there had proven to be helpful on more than a few occasions. Within seconds, he'd brought up the recent history. After another minute, he was staring at a website for adopted people—specifically women, according to the filter—who were looking for their birth parents.

Why would she be on a page like this? Did she discover she was adopted all those years ago? Had she left town to find or live with her birth mother, or something?

He leaned forward to read the heading on the page. No, the entries were all for women who were adopted in 1975. They'd all been born in the state of Texas, and all were searching for one or both of their parents.

What the hell?

Snippets of her snide comments came back to him. "You're the reason I stayed away", followed by the GI Joe comment... "You ran off when I needed you most," and most recently, "My days of needing any help from you are long gone."

Greg stared at the screen until the names began to blur. He started to shake his head, not wanting to see what was right in front of him. July 16th...all of these people... correction, all of these women were born on July 16th, thirty-one years ago. No. She wouldn't, couldn't have done that. She couldn't have had a child and given her away. Did she meet someone in California? Is that why she never came back? Something about the date jarred him...July 16th of 1975. She'd left for California over the Christmas Holidays, December 1974. A quick count on his fingers had him standing so fast the chair hit the floor with a clatter.

Several heads looked his direction as heat infused his face, his entire body.

No way. No freaking way. He bent to pick up the chair, reeling just from the thought. He shut down the computer and hurried out of the room with a quick nod to the librarian.

He'd been pounding on the door for a full minute before someone bothered to answer. It wasn't her, but her dad who finally pulled open the door.

"Hey Hart, did you come to check on the new television set? It's fine. Picture's clear as a bell but the buttons on that damn remote are too small for my clumsy fingers."

"You'll get used to it," he replied sharply. "Where the hell's Melin? I've got some questions for her." He suddenly remembered Mr. D's confession earlier about adults making wrong decisions. "Or is it you I need to talk to?" An uneasy feeling settled in his gut as Melin's father took his glasses off and wiped his eyes, looking suddenly tired and much older than his seventy something years.

"My daughter's not here, and from the look on your face, I'm thinking that's a good thing." He stepped aside and waved Greg inside. "It's time we got this out in the open. Ate at her mother and me for years. We thought we were doing her a favor, but we drove a permanent wedge between us and our only child." He pointed to one of the two matching rocker recliners. "Have a seat, Hart, and I'll tell you everything."

"I prefer to stand, but you go right ahead and sit. Just tell me why the hell Melinda was on a website for women born on July 16th, 1975, who are looking for their birth parents."

"She's looking for her daughter. She never stopped looking for her."

"Her daughter?"

"Your daughter, too, Hart."

During his entire twenty-five year stint as a Marine, he'd never had anything knock the wind out of him as those four words had. He reached for the arm of the sofa as his knees buckled. Seating himself, he rested his arms on his knees and lowered his head to keep the room from spinning.

"I've got a child? A daughter?"

"You do."

"She left town because she was pregnant with our baby. Why didn't she tell me? I would have married her. I loved her." He stood, began a steady pacing. "So instead of telling me so I could man up, she left town and then what? Gave her up for adoption? I can't believe this."

"It—it wasn't quite that simple."

Greg stopped in his tracks and turned to glare down at Melinda's father. "You'd better start talking, old man. And you'd better do it now." Mr. D. sat back in his chair and stared straight ahead, as if afraid to look him in the eye. He damned well should be.

"When my wife came to me that night, I knew by the look in her eyes something was wrong. She'd been crying, but it was more than that. She looked defeated, devastated. She'd just had a talk with Melinda and said she suspected our daughter was at least two months pregnant. We had plans for her. She was going to college, something neither of us had been able to afford. We'd scrimped and saved to put money aside for that. It was understood. We wanted her to have a real future." He sighed. "I made two phone calls that night. To a home for unwed mothers in Dallas, Texas . . . and to your parents."

Another kick to the gut.

"Are you telling me my parents knew about this?"

Mr. D. nodded. "They knew. And they knew, as my wife and I suspected, that you'd want to marry our daughter. Do the right thing—the noble thing. You'd quit your classes at the Junior college, get a job and struggle to make ends meet for the rest of your lives. We wanted better for our children than that. We wanted you both to have futures . . . careers. So, they agreed with our plan to keep it quiet."

"They knew and they kept it from me." Greg started the pacing again. "I can't wrap my head around this. It's like telling me you're from another planet. How the hell did the four of you pull this off?"

"We sent her away, Greg. We sent our only daughter away—to a place where she couldn't make a phone call that wasn't monitored, and couldn't mail a letter that wasn't read. We told them we didn't want her contacting you."

"Who came up with the California story?"

"The four of us did. We knew that neither of you would let it go unless we found a way to make you both believe you'd pushed each other aside."

"So you told me she'd lost interest and didn't want to tell me to my face, which I didn't buy at first. But when she never called, or wrote, or came home."

"You eventually accepted it."

Greg stopped in front of him. "And what did you tell Melinda, while she was over in Dallas with no one around to help her through this?"

Lawrence Dawson looked at the floor.

Greg's jaw tightened. "You told her I knew? That I didn't care?"

"At first, we didn't even bring you up. If she asked, we changed the subject. During one conversation she wouldn't let it go, and kept asking about you. We—we told her you'd been told and decided to move on."

"Son of a bitch! No wonder she can't stand the sight of me. You all told her I abandoned her, both her and our baby." He grabbed his head with both hands at the thought of what she'd gone through. "My God . . . she thinks I didn't want them." Greg began the pacing again. If he didn't move, exert some kind of energy, his heart would explode. He shook his head, still in shock over the sudden bomb-drop.

"We have a child together. We have a daughter." He stopped suddenly in the middle of his pacing. "And we wanted her, even if her grandparents didn't."

"It's not that we didn't want—"

Greg turned on him, his finger pointed in his face. "Shut up, old man! You left your own daughter to suffer through all of this alone. And you sent our daughter out into a world where God knows what happened to her. Do not try to justify any of this to me."

He swore low under his breath, furious at his own parents who'd died within four months of each other two years earlier. He threw up his hands in utter frustration. "And my parents took this crap with them to their graves, so I can't even yell at them. You'd think at least one of them would have wanted to clear their consciences after twenty-nine years." He turned on Lawrence Dawson again. "Looks like you get to shoulder the blame alone."

"It's the least I can do."

Greg nodded. "Well, finally we can agree on something. It is the very least you can do." He paced the length of the floor again, wondering if there was someone else he could blame. "Who else knew about this?"

"No one else knew."

"No one? Except for you, your wife, my parents, the other girls at the home, the nurses who practically held Melinda prisoner, the doctor who delivered our daughter, and let's not forget the child's mother, who's been searching for her for years. Searching for our child, alone, because you and three other adults thought it would be better to keep us apart with lies."

His voice caught on tears, fueled by a deeply embedded fury that threatened, at any moment, to burst forth in an agonized roar. He pressed both of his palms to his head and groaned.

"My God, what have you done to us, old man? What if she's lost to us? What if she was put in a foster home with people who abused her? What if she's dead and we never have a chance to meet her?" He turned angrily on the man. "What if she's out there somewhere, thinking her parents didn't want her and we never have the chance to tell her differently?"

"I'm sorry, Greg."

Greg erupted with a burst of hysterical laughter. "We had a saying in my unit, old man. 'Sorry don't make you any less dead'. All four of you had three decades to make it right and you didn't. You'll go to your grave, just like all the other people who claimed to have loved us, knowing you ruined three lives."

"Hart!"

Greg turned away from him. "Man, I can't talk to you anymore right now. Just tell Melin to call me when she gets home. I want to be the one to tell her I know. You owe me that much."

He heard a gurgling sound and turned back to see Melin's father clutching at his chest.

"Heart . . ." He emitted the strangled cry, just before collapsing to the floor.

Melinda pushed through the doors of the tiny hospital and headed for the nurse's station.

"Melin!"

She turned toward the voice she'd heard far more often than she'd cared to the last month or so. "What are you doing here, Gregory, and where's my dad?"

"I was with him when it happened, so I drove him here."

"What did the doctor say?" She looked around, frantic to speak to someone in charge.

"Nothing yet. We've only been here fifteen minutes."

She nodded and walked over to let the nurse know she was there. She began wearing her own path over the gray and white tiles of the waiting room floor.

She turned on Greg. "You said you were with him, so what the hell happened to bring this on? Was he trying to do too much?" The guilt-laden look he gave her made her stop her pacing to face him. "What happened?"

"We were discussing something I figured out today," he said, sounding uneasy. "Come to think of it, I was doing all the talking. He wasn't saying much of anything when it came on him."

"Were you arguing?" She was more than ready to detest him for one more reason.

Greg shoved his hands deep into his pockets. "Not exactly arguing. I—I was venting my frustration, and I said some pretty awful things to him." He put up his hand when she tried to say something. "I know about the baby, Melin. I know about our daughter."

She nodded, narrowing her eyes in ugly accusation. "So you admit that you left town in case I came back with her?"

"No, dammit! I only found out about her today. The computer in the library—I went to the browser history and accessed the last website you visited. I started putting things together, and went to confront you. Then I remembered something your dad told me the other day. Our parents kept us apart, Melin. They lied to us."

"What are you saying?"

"Your parents told me you went to California because you couldn't tell me to my face that you wanted to break up."

"What? No! That's not what happened," she stammered.

"I know that now, but for over thirty-one years I didn't."

Her eyes pooled with tears. "You didn't know I was pregnant? All this time, you didn't know I'd given birth to our child?" He took a step closer, shook his head. "I couldn't call, or write anything they didn't see first," she said, her voice thick with emotion. "A couple of times I thought I got letters out to you. Someone always found a way around things over there."

"I never got any letters, but then I never checked the mail, either. My parents would have got to it first and kept them from me." He fisted his hands and brought them to his forehead. "I can't believe they did that to us. Making you go through all of that by yourself. God, I'm so pissed, and I can't even yell at them for it."

"So you yelled at my father, instead," she accused, turning away from him.

"I did," he whispered. "I'm not proud of it, but I was bombarded by all these thoughts of what if. What if she was abused, or what if we never find her? What if she's—gone—and had to leave this earth thinking we never loved or wanted her? All our parents had a share in the blame, but he's the only one left to yell at. So, I did."

She closed her eyes, let herself relive those horrific moments. "I almost died, Greg. They wouldn't let me hold her at first. I screamed until they did. And when they pulled our baby out of my arms, I started screaming again. I screamed and fought them with everything I had. I started hemorrhaging. When things started to fade out I knew I was dying, and I was glad for it, because I had no reason to live without my baby or you."

She felt his hands light softly on her shoulders and it gave her the strength to continue. "I woke up two days later. God, I felt awful. I was so sick, Greg. Physically sick and sick at heart, too—Inside and out. They told me I'd never be able to have a child again."

Greg released a frustrated groan and turned her slowly to face him. "Something else I'm hearing for the first time. Oh, God, Melin. I'm so sorry you had to go through that alone." He wiped at the tears streaming down her face.

"Every second away from our baby broke my heart. I couldn't come home until I found her. And when that fire destroyed all the records and any traces of finding her, I couldn't come home to be around the people responsible for me losing her. Our parents lost their only children and their only chance to have a grandchild. I've never forgiven my parents, but I learned to accept it and move on. And Tiffany and Drake LeBlanc, the two children I raised in Texas, helped to fill that emptiness I felt from losing our daughter." A soft clearing of his throat reminded her she wasn't alone anymore.

"You saw her, Melin?" He whispered low and reverently.

She squeezed her eyes shut for a moment and turned slowly to face him. "I held her, Greg. Our daughter was beautiful, so tiny and pink and healthy. I may not know anything else about her, but I know this—her hair looked like it would be curly, she has my lips and nose." She gazed up at him through tear-filled eyes and raised one finger to the cleft in his chin. "And she has this."

Greg shuddered at the effort it took not to burst into tears at her words. When she reached up to brush away a single tear from his face, he grabbed her hand in his own and brought it to his mouth.

"I waited for you, Melin. I died a little each day I didn't hear from you. Finally, I couldn't stand the sight of the place. I couldn't hear one more person ask if I'd heard from you. I had to get out. I quit college and joined the Marines without even discussing it with anyone. My folks were both so pissed at me but I didn't give a rat's ass by then. I told them to forward any letters from you because I still had hopes that you'd write, and said to let me know if you called, but they never did, of course."

"It took two weeks to heal enough for them to release me. I called your house that very day, as soon as I got out of that place. Your mom told me you'd left town. I'm betting she never told you."

He shook his head. "I was already in the Marines by then, but it wouldn't have stopped me. I was stationed state side for the first year. I would have been there for you, Melin. I would have married you. We would have been together, and we would have been happy," his voice finally broke on a strangled sob as he pulled her to him. "I never stopped loving you."

The two of them stood alone in the waiting room, clinging to each other and sobbing quietly for several minutes.

"Ms. Dawson?"

They pulled apart and turned toward the voice.

"I'm Melinda Dawson. How's my father?" she asked, wiping tears from her face with the back of one hand.

"He's weak, but adamant about speaking to you. If you could keep it short. One visitor at a time," he said, when they both stepped up.

Melinda clung to Greg's hand. "He has to come with me."

He squeezed her hand, pleased more than words could say that she wanted him with her.

They stepped inside the tiny hospital's only ICU area, the steady beep of the heart monitor the only sound in the otherwise silent room. The ambulance was on its way to transfer her dad to a larger hospital with a heart unit two hours away. Judging from the ashen look on his face, Greg knew they couldn't get him there soon enough.

Melinda leaned over the bed and touched her father's face. "I'm here Dad."

He wrinkled his brow before he blinked and opened his eyes. "I don't have much time, Melinda."

"Don't you say that," she demanded, tears running down her face.

"It's okay, honey. I've lived long enough without your mother. And now that the truth is out, I can go."

"Dad . . ."

"I miss your mother, honey. We had a lot of good years together and I'm thankful for that. You staying away like you did—it forced your mom and me to be closer. But life without her—It's just not good for me. I'm ready."

"You can't leave me alone, Daddy."

He gave her a fragile smile combined with a grimace of pain. "You won't be alone, sweetheart. You and Greg. You belong together."

"Greg can't replace you," Melinda said, using the back of her hand to wipe her eyes again.

"We were wrong. Your mother and I—and Greg's parents. Never should have kept you apart. I see it now. Friggin' old age!" he gasped. "It's good for one thing. Reflecting on mistakes you've made in life." He reached out to clench her hand. "Hart still loves you. If I'm right, you feel the same way." He stiffened as pain registered on his face.

Panicked, she tried to pull her hand back to call for a nurse.

"No, I'm okay," he said. "I just—want you and Greg to find her."

Melinda choked back another sob. "I've tried Dad. The records are gone, and I can't find her."

"Keep trying until you do," he gasped again, struggling for breath before reaching out toward Greg. "Help her, Hart. Together you can. Find your daughter." He spoke in short choppy sentences that matched his hitched breathing. "Find her. Love her. Have faith. Both of you."

"Dad!" she cried, watching in horror as his eyes drifted shut. Melinda held her breath as a nurse pushed her aside to check his vitals.

Chapter 5

Melinda sat up to punch her pillow for the fifth time that night. She fell back, hoping this time would be different. She'd flip flopped on that motel bed so many times her sheets were knotted. After another five minutes she gave up the fight and flipped on her bedside lamp. She pulled a paperback from the top drawer of her nightstand and flipped it open to her bookmark. After reading the first page of the chapter for the third time, the ringing of her cell phone had her reaching to answer it, praying it wasn't bad news from the hospital.

"This is Melinda Dawson, what happened?"

"Melin, it's me."

Her head hit the pillow, her breath releasing in a rush of air. She'd nearly stroked out when her dad had simply fallen asleep on her earlier. Once he'd been transferred, his condition had immediately stabilized. "Greg? What are you doing calling at this hour? It's—" she craned her neck to check the time.

"Two o'clock in the morning, I know," he said, before she could answer. "I saw your light on and figured you were having as much trouble sleeping as I was."

"You saw my light on?" She reached over to pull the thick drapes aside, saw his truck parked outside. "Oh hell, I can't wait to hear why you're parked outside my motel room, two hours away from McCray." She waited through at least thirty seconds of tension-filled silence. "You planning to answer me in this century?"

"Take it easy on me, will you? I've been struggling to get my shit together since discovering I—that we—have a daughter."

Melinda took a deep breath and released it slowly. "Look, why don't you come on in and I'll make us some tea."

"Make it coffee and you've got a deal."

She smiled, as a sense of deja vu washed over her. They'd definitely had this conversation before, at least once and a long, long time ago. Except he hadn't asked for coffee. And she'd ended up with a lot more than a case of insomnia.

Greg walked up to the door and knocked softly. Within seconds, she'd pulled it open and waved him in. He stepped inside and closed the door behind him before meeting her green eyed gaze. God he'd loved staring into those eyes of hers, eyes that hadn't lost their appeal, even after three decades.

"Any more news on your dad?"

"Only that he was still resting comfortably." She placed a hand over heart and shook her head. "Two a.m. phone calls aren't good for much, besides scaring the hell out of me. Maybe I made a mistake giving you my number. And there are at least two dozen hotels and motels in this city. How'd you find me?"

"This is the only one near the hospital. I drove around until I saw your car. It's parked in front of this door. I've been parked out there for hours. When I saw the light come on, I took a chance. I'm sorry. I guess I shouldn't have called."

"Don't worry about it. He's fine and so am I," she said.

He felt his mouth tightening as she turned and pulled the belt of her silky robe tighter around her tiny waist. Memories washed over him, of his hands wrapped around that same waist, of pulling her close for a kiss, her arms looping around his neck, her fingers tunneling through his hair, her nails tracing enticing paths over his skin. He turned away from the sight of her preparing the coffee pot. Maybe this wasn't the best idea.

"Hey!"

Her sharp call brought his thoughts back to the present. "I'm sorry, did you say something?"

"I've only repeated the same question three times. Is regular okay? There's no decaf."

He waved it off. "I don't drink decaf."

She pushed the button on the coffee maker and turned, resting her hips against the room's entertainment center.

Her feet, covered in slippers, and crossed delicately at the ankles, drew his gaze. It travelled upward to shapely calves, firm thighs, and above. Again, a sound emitted from above his line of sight, a subtle clearing of her throat that garnered his attention. He tore his gaze away from the lower half of her body and focused on her amused expression.

"Sorry," he mumbled, as she pushed off from the dresser to enter her bathroom and close the door. He studied the emergency exit diagram hanging on the wall until she reentered the room, fully dressed in jeans, with a button down shirt. She must have seen the disappointment in his face, because she stopped, and quirked her left brow curiously. How many times had he seen her do that? Hundreds? Thousands?

"What?"

"I was hoping you still preferred letting your girls breathe while lounging around."

Melinda's lips rolled inward, as though stifling a smile before she pulled two empty mugs from the tray on top of the dresser. "Yeah, well, I wouldn't mind letting the girls breathe around others if they were still as perky as they were when I was seventeen. The sad fact is, due to the effects of gravity and time, they aren't." She poured the coffee and handed him a mug. "Things change in thirty years."

"Not from where I'm standing," he admitted. "You look better than ever, Melin." He held up a hand at her snort of disbelief. "Sure, you look more mature, but you're a perfect showcase for what we called the three 'T's' in my unit. Tanned, toned, and tempting as hell. Honestly, you look great, and it's not a line."

She lifted her filled mug in the air and gave him a smug grin. "Unless it works."

He took a moment to think about her comment then dropped his head back and groaned. "God, I can't believe you remember that."

She emitted a low chuckle. "You got me to skinny dip with that line, Gregory. It's not something I'm likely to forget," she drawled.

Greg grinned sheepishly down at her. "Yeah well, I guess it was me who introduced it to the guys in my unit." He shook his head at a distant memory. "The sight of you buck naked in that lake sort of became the benchmark for all women after that. I was a dog, wasn't I?"

She shrugged. "As far as I could tell at the time, it was only with me, and that's why your line worked. Besides—" she paused as she sipped from her cup. "You could have thrown a fourth T in there. I think I was a bit of a tease."

It was his turn to shrug. "Maybe just a little, but I should have been stronger."

"You would have held off if I'd asked you to," she said softly. "The truth is, girls that age don't realize the effect or the power they have over teen age guys. Once I realized I could make you lose control—well, it was a heady feeling. One a seventeen year old girl wasn't equipped to handle wisely."

"I was nineteen, and even less equipped to handle it—that surplus of testosterone and no outlet for it."

Her lips curled in a provocative half smile. "Oh, I don't know. From what I can remember, you were pretty well-equipped back then."

"Still am," he grunted. "Especially as far as you're concerned." Suddenly, he put the mug down on the desk and walked over to take her gently by the shoulders. "I'm so sorry, Melinda. I can't fathom what you must have been feeling. As a Marine, it shames me. As a man, it kills me that I wasn't there for you." She lowered her head and he pulled her close for a hug. They stood, rocking, swaying gently, surrounded by the generic furniture, engulfed in the deafening silence of the sleeping city.

"But you married."

"I did," he nodded. "And I loved K'Lynn but never the way she deserved to be. She sensed that I held back a part of myself—accepted it, even. She always insisted it was enough for her. She just wanted to be married, content, and have babies. And we were happy for a bit trying to get pregnant. After two years her doctor ran some tests and . . ." He shrugged and bit his lower lip.

"And they discovered the cancer. I heard. And I'm so sorry," she said. "That must have been awful for both of you."

He nodded. "She was a wonderful woman and she deserved better. Better than me as a husband, though she never complained."

Melin's brow wrinkled in concentration. "You didn't mistreat her in any way, did you?"

"Oh no—never! But I was—reserved, I guess you'd call it. My love for her wasn't borne from the same kind of passion I had with you. I guess after you, I couldn't love her the way she should have been loved."

Melinda settled her gaze onto his, the passionate pools of green holding him enthralled as they had so many years ago. He gave her lips a tentative taste, then another. The third transformed into a full buffet as she locked her lips hungrily onto his. He felt her arms loop around his neck and groaned loudly when she curled her fingers into his hair.

Sweet Jesus . . . yes. He'd skipped his last cut, hoping, praying for a moment just like this. He'd lost countless hours of sleep lately. He awakened from dreams, drenched in sweat, as though he'd really been in the back seat of that old '66 Plymouth with Melinda. His first love. His last love, if she'd have him.

She ripped his shirt out of his jeans and pulled the soft jersey over his head, moaning deep in her throat as she plastered her hands over his bare pectorals.

Never had he been so glad for his steady regimen of running and weight lifting to keep in shape. With shaky hands, he cupped her shoulders then ran both hands up her neck to either side of her face, pulling her close for a soul-searing kiss.

Before he knew it, she'd tugged his belt open, unsnapped his jeans and was working with agile fingers on his zipper. With a rush of breath he pulled her hands away. "Wait."

"I don't want to wait another second. Not one more second for you, Gregory."

He grinned down at her. "You know, you're the only person in the world who ever got away with calling me that."

"Is that so?" she breathed, pulled him close to nibble on his ear.

He released a low chuckle. "Uh huh. Now, stop that, Melin. We need to talk."

She groaned as he pulled her away from him and sat her on the bed. He sat beside her, taking her left hand in his own. "I've been thinking about this moment since you walked into my store for those triple-A batteries, lady."

Her free hand stroked softly down one side of his face. "You have?"

"Yep, and I don't want to mess it up, so bear with me, all right?" He waited until she seemed to digest his words and gave him a silent nod.

"I want you, Melin. But not until you know how I feel. I guess God had a reason for making things turn out the way they did. I guess we were meant to meet different people along the way." He shook his head slowly. "But, I feel like we've had the majority of our lives stolen from us."

"Three decades," she agreed.

He nodded. "I've been thinking that maybe getting back on track will help us to heal from this faster."

"What do you mean back on track?"

Greg pulled a small box out of his pocket and held it in front of her. He stared into the face of the woman he'd been in love with for so many years. Her cheeks flushed a becoming rose color the second she saw the box.

"I've held onto this for nearly thirty-two years." He opened the box to reveal a delicate ring, a single tiny diamond, paired with emeralds on either side of it, all set in gold.

She raised her gaze to his, and blinked several times to keep her tears at bay. "You bought this for me?"

He nodded. "I'd planned to give it to you for Christmas your senior year but you were gone by then." He took the ring from the box and smiled. "I had my speech all prepared too, only I never got to deliver it." He leaned back and held the ring out to her. "So, does this look like something you'd want to hang onto?"

"Surely you had a better speech prepared than that?" she murmured, eyeing the ring longingly.

"I did."

She cocked her head playfully and sat back on the bed. "Well, I believe I've earned the right to hear it."

Several seconds and a few nervous throat clearings later, Greg began to speak. "I remember the first day I saw you, Melinda. It was your first day of kindergarten and you were trying to comfort your mother. You told her you wanted to walk in alone your first day of school." He gave a low chuckle at the memory. "Your poor mom was a basket case. Do you remember that?"

She nodded. "I finally had to tell her she could come with me so she'd quit crying."

He nodded. "Yep, you did, and I remember thinking that you must be the strongest little girl in the whole world. And me being an 'older man' of seven, I'd already seen plenty of girls by then to compare you to."

"Well sure, you being a mature second grader, man of the world, and all," she agreed.

"You got it, so even at such an early age I knew what I wanted in a woman. Strength, independence, and even at five, I knew you'd be a looker."

"What gave it away, my face full of freckles or my banged up knees?"

He passed a finger lovingly over the light spattering of freckles across the bridge of her nose. "The sparkle in those gorgeous green eyes of yours, Melin. They always could see clear into my soul."

He slipped to one knee before her and heard her breath hitch as he removed the ring from its velvet pillow. "Melinda Denise Dawson," he said softly. "Would you do me the honor of marrying me?"

She caressed his face and beamed. "I believe I will, Gregory."

"I'll exchange this diamond for something bigger, but I wanted you to see it in its original form, first. It's all I could afford at the time."

She smiled. "I would have loved it then. And I love it now, bigger diamond or no."

"Good to know." He slipped the ring onto her left ring finger. "One thing, though. After we're married you're gonna have to nix the Gregory thing. Call me Greg like everyone else. Either that, or love of your life, or your highness, or something equally befitting."

"Aw," she drawled. "It's so cute that you think you'll ever be able to tell me what to do."

He kissed the finger he'd just slipped the ring onto and smiled. "Nothing but attitude." Melinda's soft laughter had him smiling again.

"I'm too set in my ways to change now," she said. "You'll just have to get used to my lip."

"I love your lip. As a matter of fact, I love both your lips." He pushed her gently back on the bed and stretched out beside her. "Are you going to make me wait for you, Melin?"

"Wait for what?"

"To start our life together. To marry me."

"I think we've both waited long enough, don't you? As soon as Dad's out of the woods, I'll start thinking about that. Is that satisfactory, Gregory?"

He supported himself with one elbow as he reached down to unbutton her shirt. "Sounds like a plan. But if it's okay with you, I'd like to start the reacquainting process immediately."

She smiled. "Just as soon … we're not getting any younger, after all."

They slipped off the rest of their clothes and he helped her lose the bra, baring her beautiful pale globes to him. They lay there facing each other while he studied her still sexy as hell body. He traced an obvious tan line both above and below her breasts, evidence of her life in sunny southeast Texas. "Does this mean you don't do much skinny dipping back in the lone star state?"

"This girl always wears a swimsuit. Still a two-piece, though at my age, a bit more modest than the bikinis I once wore." She smiled suggestively. "I can tell you I've only skinny-dipped once in my life."

He stared at her, wide-eyed and amazed at her confession. "Seriously?"

Her eyes fluttered closed when he trailed his hand along the outside of her breast. "Mmmm—uh huh. Yours was the only line I ever heard that worked on me. After all I'd been through, I was immune to the whisperings of any other good-looking, sexy men with one thing on their minds."

"Nice to know you found me good-looking and sexy—and you're totally correct about me having one thing on my mind. You were all I could think about back then, right up until I joined the Corps. After that they worked me too hard to think about much else. For a few minutes, just before falling into an exhausted sleep, I could picture you gloriously naked beneath me. But that hurt too much because I'd start imagining you gloriously naked beneath some guy you'd met in California."

"Not true," she murmured.

"I know that now but then I didn't know anything more than what our parents told me." He leaned over her, took one nipple gently into his mouth, rolling it around his tongue. He smiled at her hiss of breath when he released it slowly. "The day you walked into my shop—back into my life—it started up all over again. You're like an invasion—a hostile one, at that." Greg cupped her breast in one hand, slipped his other between her legs. He blew on her nipple, groaned at his fiancée's intake of breath as he found her slick core, pressing with the pad of his thumb. The simultaneous tightening of her nipple and nub, along with her low groan of appreciation, nearly proved too much for him.

"Enough, Gregory. Trust me—I'm ready for you."

He looked around at their surroundings. He hadn't exactly imagined this happening at a motel around the corner of a hospital. "Are you sure? I'd pictured making it a little more special for you."

Her green-eyed gaze zeroed in on him. "Our parents robbed us of thirty years—this will happen tonight." She shifted so that she straddled him. "This will happen now." She raised herself above him and settled into position with a long, slow sigh. "Oh . . . my . . ."

Greg didn't dare close his eyes, unwilling to lose sight of her for a second. He watched as she rode him, amazed at how good—how right it felt to be with her again. He cupped Melin's two breasts, thrilled at the weight of them in his hands—slightly fuller, heavier, but still perky despite her earlier comments about time and gravity taking their toll on her. She'd matured in thirty years, of course, but her body still turned him on as it had at seventeen.

He wrapped his hands around her slim waist, noting as he pulled her down hard onto him how perfectly they fit. Her eyes flew open at his actions and he stared into the green depths, wondering how he'd lived without her all these years. Her breasts called to him and he reached up to cup them again, drawing slow circles with his thumbs on her nipples. She closed her eyes, letting her head fall back as she groaned low in her throat. Greg grabbed her hips and pulled down hard until she cried out with her release. He struggled to maintain as she leveled off, coming down slowly—waited until she'd achieved every moment of pleasure she could before he let himself go with a guttural groan.

She collapsed on him afterwards, lay there gasping for breath. "Oh, God, that was amazing."

"Sure as hell was," he said, the combination of their accelerated heartbeats pounding like kettle drums against his chest. He held her close, thinking it had been more than amazing—it had been like coming home. "I love you so much, Melinda."

"I love you too, Gregory."

He placed one hand on her head, wove his fingers through her silky waves. The action brought back memories of him doing that very thing dozens, if not hundreds of times over the year they'd dated. He finally had her back in his life and he'd damned sure keep her there.

"Now this," he spoke softly into her hair. "This is back on track."

"Mmm … absolutely," she replied in a tone more purred than spoken.

"I hope you don't mind, but I'd like to make one more suggestion," he countered.

She raised her head, her green eyes wide, staring curiously at him. "Suggestion? Are we talking form or technique?"

He grinned. "Neither, honey. Every second of that was perfection. But I'd like to hold off on making love with you again until our wedding night." He chuckled at the frown pulling on the corners of her mouth. "What's wrong, babe? Don't think you can keep your hands off of me for that long?"

Her lips rounded in a shocked gasp, and she pushed up and away from him. She sat there beside him, staring down, her brows arched at the challenge. "Wow, Hart—are you full of yourself, or what?"

Memories of the few times she'd called him by his last name came to mind—and not in a good way. "I haven't heard that tag in that tone since I asked Tabitha Green to my senior prom."

"Because you waited until after she'd won the title of Miss McCray," Melinda said, tight-lipped.

"In all fairness, I only asked Tabbie because I couldn't ask you."

"And why not? The school had no rules about sophomores going to prom."

"But your dad did. He told me not to bother asking you."

"You spoke to my dad?"

"Yes, and he said you weren't allowed to date until your junior year."

"Oh. Well, now I feel really bad. I kinda mentioned to a few people that you only asked her because of her reputation."

"She had a reputation?"

Melinda rolled her eyes. "She slept with a couple of the contest's male judges. She's the reason they switched to female judges after that."

"Really . . ." he mused, scratching his chin. "And here I was, feeling slighted because they didn't ask me to judge the contest last year."

"Now you know," she said, shooting him a side-eyed glance. "Was I really your first choice for prom?"

"Yep…ask your dad." He smoothed her curls back from her forehead and cupped her face between both hands. "You've always been my first choice, Melin. Didn't you know that? Do you honestly think I'd have chosen a career as a Marine over you?"

She blinked several times as tears filled her beautiful eyes. "We were robbed of so many years, Greg. Neither of us questioned our parents. Thinking back on it now, I wonder why I didn't. I never doubted our love for each other before then."

"We were both raised to respect our parents. We just didn't expect them to make such monumental mistakes. Mistakes three of them took to their graves."

She sniffed and curled once more against his side, her head resting on his chest. "I have to find a way to forgive them. I don't want to waste another thirty years with that anger inside me."

"How about if we replace our anger with determination," he suggested. "Determination to find our daughter."

She traced circular patterns in the hair on his chest. "Do you really think we can? I've come up against so many dead ends."

He pulled his fingers to his lips and kissed them. "This time you'll have me to help you."

"And what if we never find her?"

Her quiet sniffling had him pulling her close. "Then we'll have each other, babe. For the rest of our lives, through thick or thin, Melin. We'll have each other."

Chapter 6

"You want another cup of coffee, Cyn?" Melinda asked her friend.

Cynthia finished wrapping the last of Melinda's plates and stacked it neatly inside the moving box. "Only if I can have it with another of those fruit tarts."

"Sure." Melinda slid a large plastic container across the counter top. "Pick your poison."

Cyn examined the contents of the container. "Got any strawberry tarts left?"

"If I do, it's got an X marked on the crust. Good luck, though. Those are Greg's favorites."

"A ha!" Cyn held up a tart in victory. "He must have missed one." She took a bite and rolled her eyes blissfully. "God, these things are so good, Melin. Have you thought any more about buying the bakery? I swear you'd make a killing."

"Actually, I've spoken to Mr. Lee about it and I told him I'd buy the building if he gave me six months. I don't want to start my marriage fighting to get a new business off the ground."

"I hear you. I doubt you'll have to struggle. Hell, there's nothing else left around here. You won't have any problems making a go of it."

"I hope you're right, my friend," Melinda huffed as she hauled a step stool to the pantry. "If I haven't told you this before, I appreciate you helping me get this place packed up." She shook her head. "I never realized two old people could collect so much stuff. I have to get this placed emptied before the wedding in two weeks. I have some potential buyers coming to look at it whenever I give them the word."

"I think you two made the right choice. Selling both your places to buy something new. No ghosts from either house. Fresh starts for both of you."

Melinda climbed up on the stepladder to reach the top shelf. "I'll be damned! There's more of mom's preserves shoved way to the back up here. At least a dozen more jars."

"Hey, you've hit the mother lode!" Cyn exclaimed, reaching for some of the jars Melinda handed down to her. "There's something stuck to the bottom of that quart jar you just picked up."

Melinda stepped down from the ladder before checking it out. She pulled what was left of a pad of post it notes from the bottom of the jar and sat down to examine it. "Looks like a shopping list—" She stopped short.

"For what?"

Melinda could feel the ear to ear grin spreading across her face, even as her eyes clouded with tears. "Oh Cyn! It's mom's recipe." She looked up, her heart filled with joy. "For her strawberry preserves."

"Her prize-winning strawberry preserves?" Cynthia's voice hushed with reverence.

Melinda nodded. "Yep." She sniffed loudly as she wiped away her trail of tears. "Thanks Mom," she whispered, holding the notepad close to her heart. "You're covered when it comes to wedding gifts."

Epilogue

Wedding Cookies

1 1/2 cups unsalted butter
3/4 cup confectioners sugar
3/4 tsp. salt
1 1/2 cups finely ground almonds
4 1/2 tsps. vanilla extract
3 cups sifted all-purpose flour
1/3 cup confectioners' sugar (for rolling)

Preheat oven to 365 degrees.

Cream butter in a bowl. Gradually add confectioners' sugar and salt. Beat until light and fluffy. Add almonds and vanilla. Blend in flour gradually and mix well.

Shape into balls, using about 1 tsp. for each cookie. Place on ungreased cookie sheets and bake for 15-20 minutes. Do not brown. Cool slightly and roll in confectioners' sugar.

Melinda stared at her beaming reflection in the mirror. She smoothed the waist of her fitted gown, wondering when she'd ever had so much to smile about. A light knock on the door had her walking over to see who it was. She pulled it open cautiously, determined not to let her future husband see her dress, in case it was him. "Is that you, Gregory?"

"Did someone ask for a doctor?"

Air rushed from Melinda's lungs as she threw the door open. "Tiffany! How did you know?"

The young blonde with large brown eyes laughed as her Nanny nearly squeezed the life out of her. "Greg called last week and asked us to keep it a surprise for you."

"Us? Are you telling me Drake's here, too?"

"Of course I am."

She spun around to take in the sight of the tall, good-looking young man standing in the doorway. Despite the sandy brown hair that would curl if left long enough, his facial features resembled his sister's. Three years younger than Tiffany, he'd inherited both his father's height and athletic build.

"My favorite counselor!" Melinda threw her arms around him for a hug then stood back, gazing at the two young people she'd practically raised solely since they were infants. "I can't believe you both came."

"I can't believe you'd think we wouldn't, Melin," Drake said. "You're the nearest thing to a mother we've ever had."

"At least one that liked us," Tiffany added.

Melinda placed gentle caresses on each of their faces and smiled through tear-filled eyes. "I couldn't love you two kids more if you were my own."

Greg listened to the exchange with a sense of extreme satisfaction. Somehow, despite their hectic schedules, Melinda's two "kids" managed to pull off their surprise visit without a hitch. It was just one more way he'd spend the rest of his life making up for lost time with Melinda. He finally gave his throat a loud clearing.

"If that's you, Gregory, don't you come in here."

"I wouldn't dare, babe, and I hate to cut your reunion short but Father Carlos says it's time to get started."

Melinda gave a squeal of delight. "Are you ready for this?"

He grinned at her enthusiasm. "I have been for a while."

"Thank you for calling my kids, Greg."

"I didn't want you to walk up the aisle alone, and now you've got some company. I love you, Melin, and I'll see you in a bit."

Greg walked briskly through the long hallway that brought him to the front of the church. He took his place in front of the altar, standing straight and tall, and waited, never more anxious to see the love of his life than he was at this moment.

The strains of Pachelbel's Canon in D began slowly, gradually filling the air with a multitude of strings. When the double doors finally opened, the music swelled, drowning out the appreciative gasps and comments of the two hundred or so guests filling the church. The photographer snapped pictures, blocking his view of the woman he wanted to spend the rest of his life with. Finally, the way cleared and he caught his first sight of her. He nearly choked on his own gasp of prideful appreciation at the beauty before him, draped in antique lace and satin.

She walked slowly to him, flanked on either side by Tiffany and Drake LeBlanc, both beaming with pride at their assigned duties. That plan had come to fruition beautifully, adding to the sheer look of joy on Melin's face.

Totally worth it.

He knew her father's death two months earlier had weighed heavily on his fiancée. Her dad's last wishes were that they go through with the wedding plans. "No more waiting for each other…" had been his last words before closing his eyes for good.

She took an agonizingly long time to reach him before shedding her escorts with warm hugs and tearful kisses. When she finally turned and focused on him, his heart nearly exploded with the happiness he felt.

"Finally. You're here. And you're breathtaking," he whispered.

She beamed up at him, her eyes sparkling with happy tears. "Thank you, Greg. I love you so very much."

He reached out with both hands to cup her face. "I love you too, and before we get started, I want to make this solemn promise to you." His words were quiet, sounding almost sacred considering their location. "I vow to find our daughter, Melinda. If it takes every penny we have and up to my dying breath, I'll find her."

Melinda reached up and placed a hand on his cheek. "We'll find her, all right. But we'll find her together. Are you ready?"

He grinned, taking her hand and tucking it lovingly under his arm. "As I've ever been for anything. Let's do this."

Thank you so much for letting me share Melinda and Greg's story with you. Please consider leaving me a review at your favorite e-book retailer and/or Goodreads. Reviews are a writer's best friend. Even the bad ones if they're constructive. Merci beaucoup! (Thank you, very much!)

~Lori Leger

Lori Leger

3 Series...3 Ways to Feel the Love

La Fleur de Love series

HALOS & HORNS series

Other books by LORI LEGER

La Fleur de Love Series
Book 1: Some Day Somebody
Book 2: Last First Kiss
Book 2.5: Hart's Desire (Novella)
Book 3: Brown Eyed Girl
Book 4: Heaven in Your Eyes

Halos & Horns Series
Book 1: Green Eyed Temptation
Book 2: Sarah Smile
Book 3: Meagan's Marine
Book 4: One Year to Forever
Book 5: Tinseled Up in Texas

Prime of Love Series
Book 1: Running Out of Rain
Book 2: Hanging On To Hope
Book 3: Settling For More

Seasons of Love Series
Book 1: Hearts, Hearths & Holidays
Book 2: Spring Promise
Book 3: Sweet Summertime Love
Book 4: Christmas by Candlelight
Book 5: It's a Summer Thing

Full Circle Love: Combined short stories from Seasons of Love series (Books 2-5) involving Cathryn and Zachary.

Christmas 911: A Christmas novel published with The Wild Rose Press

About the Author

Award winning author, Lori Leger, adores writing stories set in southwest Louisiana, where good Cajun cooking, helping your neighbors, and saying 'y'all' is as normal as hurricanes, heat, and humidity. She has twelve full-length novels, and five short stories published in four series: La Fleur de Love, its spin-off, Halos & Horns, Seasons of Love, Prime of Love series, one stand-alone Christmas suspense published with The Wild Rose Press, with two more in production and if God is willing, more to come.

She's contributed to the Sweet & Savory Cookbook of Amazon Authors, published by Top Ten Press. Lori also has an article published in the non-fiction book Writing After Retirement: Tips From Retired Writers, published by Rowman and Littlefield Publishers, and edited and compiled by Carol Smallwood and Christine Redman-Waldeyer.

Her fourth novel in the Halos & Horns series, "One Year to Forever" won 2015 Romance Novel of Excellence award from InD'tale Review magazine.